FALLING FOR
THE PREGNANT
HEIRESS

FALLING FOR THE PREGNANT HEIRESS

SUSAN MEIER

MILLS & BOON

First published in Great Britain 2019
by Mills & Boon, an imprint of HarperCollins*Publishers*
1 London Bridge Street, London, SE1 9GF

Large Print edition 2019

© 2019 Linda Susan Meier

ISBN: 978-0-263-08310-1

MIX
Paper from
responsible sources
FSC® C007454

This book is produced from independently certified FSC™ paper to ensure responsible forest management. For more information visit www.harpercollins.co.uk/green.

Printed and bound in Great Britain
by CPI Group (UK) Ltd, Croydon, CR0 4YY

To my bowling buddies
on the Tuesday afternoon league.

We may not always bowl well,
but we laugh a lot!

CHAPTER ONE

ANYONE WHO LOOKED at Sabrina McCallan usually did a double take. With her blond hair, blue eyes and nicely kept curves, she was physically perfect. Add impeccable manners, poise, charm, grace and intelligence, and Trent "Ziggy" Sigmund thought the woman was class in Chanel.

Until today.

As a bridesmaid in her brother Seth's August wedding, standing by a church pew, waiting for her turn in the after-ceremony pictures, she seemed frazzled. Nervous. Plus, a strand of yellow hair had sprung from her up-do and she hadn't tucked it back in.

Which was why Trent couldn't stop staring at her.

Sabrina's partner in Seth and Harper's wedding, Trent was supposed to be aware of where Sabrina was when their names were called for the pictures, and her fidgeting confused him. He wasn't staring because he was attracted to her. She wasn't his type. She was perfect, flawless, and he liked things a little messy. Not a disaster. But wild hair on a pillow, sleepy eyes, torn jeans and scruffy tennis shoes were more his speed.

Still, something was up with Sabrina and he had responsibilities as her partner in the wedding, more as her brother's best friend. He and Seth had lived together in a run-down apartment, both earning their living as waiters, as they finished school. They'd shared spare change and food, knew the bus and subway schedules like the backs of their hands and played wingman when one or the other spotted a girl they liked. Though Seth had dropped out of his family for a time, the second McCallan son still knew "people" and that had helped Trent get his first job, which had resulted in his learning the right things at the right time to develop his genius, strike out on his own and become rich.

In some ways they were like brothers. In other ways they were closer than brothers.

Trent would be a fool if he didn't realize he owed Seth. And Trent wasn't a fool.

Which was why Seth's little sister's fidgeting was like a red alert alarm. The groom, Seth, was too busy to notice. Even Jake, Seth and Sabrina's older brother, was busy with his toddler and pregnant wife. Only Trent had time to see the McCallan daughter was off her game today.

When his name and Sabrina's were called for their picture, Trent sauntered across the church aisle to stunning Sabrina. Her pale purple dress highlighted her blue eyes. Her yellow hair would have been perfection, except for that one wayward strand, which to Trent's way of thinking, actually made her more beautiful.

He offered his arm. The way he and Sabrina had grown up might have been worlds apart, but twelve years of knowing a McCallan had taught him how a gentleman behaved.

"Ready for pics?"

Sabrina smiled politely as she slid her hand into the crook of his elbow. "Yes."

He nearly told her she looked elegant and feminine in the simple lilac dress Harper had chosen for her bridesmaids, but he figured she'd probably heard that thirty or forty times already today.

They walked to the space the photographer pointed out, stood by Seth and Harper and smiled as the middle-aged man snapped a picture. He took at least a hundred more shots with Seth and Harper and the members of their bridal party, Harper's parents, Seth's mom Maureen, Seth's brother Jake and his wife, Avery, and then a few final shots of everyone—a big mob of men in tuxes, women in gowns and little girls in dresses with so much tulle and ruffles, Trent wondered how they could stay upright.

Seth's mom and Harper's parents said their goodbyes. Harper's parents were taking Harper's daughter, Crystal, home for a nap before the reception. Seth's mom was going home for a nap herself. Jake and Avery's nanny hustled Abby to their Upper East Side condo for some quiet time. The rest of the wedding party took limos to Seth and Harper's penthouse for a few pre-reception drinks.

Thanking everyone for joining him in the celebration of the happiest day of his life, Seth popped the cork on the first bottle of champagne, then servants scurried over to open more champagne, fill glasses and distribute them for a toast.

Leaning against the bar, Trent kept his attention on Sabrina. She took a glass of champagne, happily raised it when best man Jake made a toast, then pretended to sip.

Trent's eyes narrowed. She had absolutely *pretended* to sip. Three toasts later, she still had a full glass of champagne.

The bride and groom mingled through the small crowd. Waiters brought out trays of hors d'oeuvres. Seth told stories of his misspent youth, and with Harper by his side, he spoke fondly of her deceased husband, Clark, the third roommate in the trio of Clark, Seth and Ziggy, who now preferred to be called Trent. Trent joined him in one final story. Then the conversation drifted to more current topics, and before Trent knew it, it was time to go to the Waldorf Astoria for the reception.

He had to hunt for Sabrina. When he found her, she looked to have gotten lost in the shuffle. A woman who ran a nonprofit that helped startups turn into corporations did not get lost in any shuffles.

He added her obvious confusion to her not drinking and came up with a conclusion so startling it almost made him whistle—the way his stepfather always had when he realized something outlandish, something farfetched, something so out of the realm of reality that only a physical gesture or a reverently whispered "Wow" would do.

Sabrina held up as well as she could through the small party at Seth and Harper's. When Ziggy found her—again—to ride with her to the reception, she wanted to throttle him. She needed some alone time to figure things out and her brother's best friend, her groomsman partner, always seemed to be two feet away.

She'd think he'd suddenly gotten a thing for her, but she knew better. If the wild-haired waifs he dated were anything to go by, she wasn't his type. But he wasn't her type, either. He was good-looking enough. His black hair curled into sexy ringlets on his collar. His heavy-lidded dark eyes never missed a thing. But he was scruffy. He liked things like dimly lit jazz bars and kicking back with a beer by the lake. Any lake. She was pretty sure he owned houses on three of them.

Then there was his name. She'd never get used to calling him Trent. First, because her brother had called him Ziggy for at least a decade. Second, because to her the name Ziggy fit the laid-back billionaire much more than Trent.

And nobody really wanted to be dating a guy named Ziggy, let alone a high-profile professional woman. She ran a respectable nonprofit. Her public persona determined whether she got contributions and grants to assist the hundreds of people who came to her with ideas every year.

Trent helped her into one of the black limos that had pulled up to the curb in front of Seth and Harper's building.

She smiled politely. "Thank you."

"You're welcome."

The driver closed the door behind them, walked to the front of the long car and took his seat behind the steering wheel.

Trent pushed the button that raised the glass between passengers and the driver. "Are you okay?"

"What? Yes! I'm fine."

"Nothing you want to tell me?"

She gave him the side eye. "Of course not."

"I'm just saying you look like a woman who might need a shoulder to cry on or maybe somebody to offer advice."

She fought the urge to close her eyes and kept her poise strictly intact. He couldn't know that she was pregnant. *She'd* only found out that morning. One stupid week of loneliness had her flying off to Paris to Pierre—with whom she'd made the mutual decision to break up the month before—and spending a reckless weekend that resulted in a child.

She'd sensed a bit of regret on Pierre's part when she'd left to return to New York, but not enough for him to call her. Which was for the best. As a woman who didn't believe in love, she'd accepted Pierre's romantic advances four years ago because she knew there was no danger that anything would come of their affair. A gorgeous, passionate artist, Pierre was a lot of fun and they spoke the language of art. They both lived and breathed art. But Pierre was the product of a marriage more dysfunctional than Sabrina's parents' marriage had been, and he'd decided to make up for his parents' neglect by giving himself everything he wanted. He'd also taken a solemn vow never to marry or have kids. Which was okay because they weren't long-term anything. They had a safe, long-distance relationship, with no possibility of things getting messy with talk of love.

And now that she was pregnant?

Well…

They'd broken up. He didn't want to be a father. She'd never wanted him in her life permanently. Nothing had changed.

At least she didn't think so. But that was the problem. There hadn't yet been time to think this through. She hadn't had two quiet minutes since she'd seen the stick turn blue, and her nerves were beginning to fray. Part of her wanted to enjoy her brother's big day and celebrate. The other part wanted to go home and cry. Except—

She didn't know if she wanted to cry out of fear or happiness. She'd always wanted to be a mom. She'd envisioned herself having as close of a relationship with her child as she'd had with her mom, guiding her little boy or girl into a wonderful, fulfilling life, choosing good schools, taking her baby to the park, maybe even getting a dog—

She'd just always thought it would be some-time in the future.

"I'm fine."

"Okay. Keep your secrets."

An arrow plunged into her heart, scaring her to death at the way he'd made *secret* plural. *Secrets.* Being pregnant wasn't her only secret. She also painted. Temperamental, brilliant Pierre was one of a handful of people who knew Sabrina McCallan was the reclusive art-ist Sally McMillan. She'd taken a pseudonym because as Sabrina McCallan she was New York high society. Her one and only showing had been mobbed by people buying her paint-ings to win favor with her now-deceased ty-coon father.

She'd been on the verge of quitting painting altogether when her mother had suggested a pseudonym. And it worked. She didn't go to her showings, didn't schmooze or pander to the public. Her art stood on its own.

Still, Ziggy couldn't know that. Seth, Jake, Avery and Harper all knew the stakes. Seth would not have spilled her secret. None of them would.

Ziggy was bluffing.

"Maybe I should ask you if *you* need some counseling."

He laughed.

She lifted one eyebrow. "Afraid your business won't stand up to the scrutiny of a professional?"

"Honey, my business wouldn't stand up to anybody's scrutiny. I have a couple simple formulas. I read five newspapers a day and a few dozen blogs. Once I get all the information I need in my head, I grab a fishing pole and go to the lake, or I slip off to Spain and let it all sink in. After a few days I might make a move, or I might not."

"That's really not a business."

"Didn't I just say that?"

The train of limos arrived at the Waldorf. Doormen scurried out to release the passengers and escort the bridal party into the hotel. When Sabrina and Ziggy arrived at the four-story, two-tiered ballroom, the place was lit with dim purple lights that made the space shimmer romantically. Long, rectangular tables outlined the room, while round, more intimate tables filled the area beside the open dance floor.

Sabrina murmured, "This is lovely."

Ziggy looked around. "Your family does know how to throw a party."

His casual way of looking at things hit her all the wrong ways. "We aren't throwing a party. We're celebrating a marriage."

"Potayto, potahto."

"It's not the same thing! A party can be four guys and a beer bong. We're celebrating my brother and his wife finding love."

He faced her with a goofy smile, his dark eyes gleaming with mischief. "You're a romantic."

She almost laughed. Her? A romantic? She was exactly the opposite. She was a woman who believed romance and the mythical concept of "love" only caused problems—especially for women. She would never let herself be so vulnerable as to fall in love.

"I'm not a romantic. You know as well as anyone that our family had a rough time." A dad who couldn't be faithful and a mom with three kids who lived in fear of his temper. "I never thought either of my brothers would get married."

Ziggy nodded. "Yeah. I guess you're right."

She straightened to her full five feet six inches—five-nine with heels—and still she only came up to about his nose. Odd that she'd notice that with so much on her mind. "You're damned right, I'm right. Now, if you'll excuse me, don't follow me to the ladies' room."

He laughed.

She strode away, feeling more like herself than she had all day. There was nothing like righting a wrong to get her blood flowing. Having her spunk back helped her to weed through some of the confusion in her brain.

Number one, she wanted the baby. Because of her parents' abysmal marriage, she'd vowed never to marry, but she wanted to be a mother. This pregnancy might have sped up her time-table, but she was ready—

No. She was *eager* to become a mom.

Number two, she had to tell Pierre. She expected him to be appalled and tell her that he wanted nothing to do with their child. But she'd chosen him as a lover, someone with no intention of falling in love, not a father for her children, so that was okay. She had no qualm about raising this baby alone. In fact, she'd prefer it.

Number three and four, telling her mom and telling her brothers couldn't happen until she told Pierre.

She had to go to Paris.

She walked into the elegant lounge section of the ladies' room and leaned across a vanity to get a peek at her makeup. Now that she wasn't falling apart internally, her face had gone back to normal. She could have nitpicked every tiny imperfection. She could have second-guessed her choice of lipstick color. Except she looked like the lady her mother had raised her to be. She might not be perfect, but she was firmly in her role.

She drew a long breath and left the restroom, heading back to the ballroom. She spotted Ziggy and walked in the opposite direction. Jake was about to introduce Seth and Harper and the bridal party. She ambled up to Harper, who looked elegant in her simple satin dress. Her short, dark hair gave her the look of a pixie. Her blue eyes sparkled with love— for Sabrina's brother. Sabrina could never appreciate anyone more than she did Avery and Harper for helping her brothers to heal. Theirs were the rare unicorn of relationships that did revolve around love, exactly what her brothers needed.

But Sabrina didn't need to heal as her brothers had. A daughter, not a son, she hadn't endured the kind of cruel mistreatment from their dad that her brothers had. Her chauvinistic father didn't see her as a businesswoman, so he had no reason to "train" her. But she had seen how he treated her mom, how her mom had cried over his infidelities and worried for her sons. At fourteen, Sabrina had promised herself no man would ever treat her the way her dad had treated her mom. And she'd kept that promise.

"Anything I can do for the bride?"

Harper hugged her. "No. We're fine. I'd just like to get to dinner already. I'm starved."

"You should have had some hors d'oeuvres at your penthouse. They were wonderful."

"I was saving my appetite for the Beef Wellington."

As Jake began announcing the wedding party, Ziggy walked up to her and escorted her to her seat. Jake then introduced himself and his wife, Avery, who joined him by the podium. He introduced Seth and Harper and the room broke into joyous applause.

Tears filled her eyes. She really couldn't express how grateful she was to her two sisters-in-law for saving her brothers, healing them, helping them to believe in love and lead normal, happy lives.

Harper finally got her Beef Wellington and the dinner progressed with Ziggy making small talk with her one minute and turning to his left to talk to her mother the next. She supposed he was an okay guy—

All right. He was sort of a great guy, considerate of her and kind to her mother. She shouldn't have snapped at him.

She never snapped at anyone.

But there was something about Ziggy today. Something about the sexy way he looked in a tux—or maybe the way he'd asked if she needed someone to talk to—

She didn't know. Her hormones were a mess and so were her reactions. But now that she'd worked everything out in her head, she could get back to normal.

The band announced Seth and Harper's first dance, and her brother escorted his bride to the dance floor. When the music ended, the band announced Jake and Avery, who joined Seth and Harper, then Trent and Sabrina, who walked out onto the dance floor with them.

The band began a slow, romantic song for the bridal party dance, and Sabrina drew a quiet breath. Trent slid his arm around her waist. She put her hand on his shoulder—his very solid shoulder.

That was a surprise. Pierre was a tall, thin man, and touching someone more solid sent a jolt through her. She hadn't expected Ziggy to be buff.

"Do you work out?"

He waggled his eyebrows. "Liking my muscles?"

She rolled her eyes. "Can you be serious for one second?"

"I tried to be serious in the limo. You shut me down."

"You weren't being serious. You were prying into my life."

"See, there you go again. Making distinctions that don't need to exist."

The music shifted into something faster for mere seconds, but Trent took advantage of those seconds to spin them around. Silly though it was, the movement lightened her mood. She laughed.

"See? That's what I wanted to hear. A laugh. A spontaneous one at that."

She shook her head. "You're weird."

"No. We're opposites."

She inclined her head in agreement.

"Which means if you told me whatever was troubling you, I'd come up with an out-of-the-box solution that might help you."

This time she didn't try to deny that she was in the throes of figuring out a problem. "You can't help me."

Her honesty surprised Trent. Not only did it mean she trusted him, but also, he'd never been able to do a real, solid favor for Seth. The McCallans wanted for nothing. If he could do something kind for the sister of the guy who'd given him the boost he'd needed to become the success he was, he was at her beck and call. "You're so sure."

She looked away. "Yeah." She caught his gaze. "Can you keep a secret?"

Without hesitation Trent said, "Absolutely."

"There's not really anything you can do about the fact that I'm pregnant."

Trent didn't react. He'd already guessed that. "I have three getaway houses in the US and a condo in Spain. I have a yacht that's really nice for privacy when you need it. If nothing else, let me give you a place to think this through."

She caught his gaze. "I don't need to think it through. I need to go to France to tell the baby's dad. I can't use one of the McCallan jets because my family will know where I've gone. And I don't want them to know." She bit her lower lip. "At least not yet. I have to tell the baby's father before I tell my family."

He perked up. "I have three jets."

Her blue eyes filled with hope. "You'd lend me one?"

"Sure."

The hope in her eyes turned to skepticism as the song ended. "And you wouldn't tell Seth?"

He made a cross on his chest. "I'll keep all of this a secret until you have a chance to tell everyone yourself. When do you need the jet?"

"Tonight."

"So soon?"

"I just want to get this over with. You know, get myself moving forward again."

He tucked his hands in his trouser pockets. "Okay. I'd give you the keys, but if jets have keys I'm pretty sure my pilot has them."

She laughed and impulsively hugged him. "Thanks."

The strangest feelings rattled through Trent. She was softer than he'd thought she'd be. Of course, he rarely dated women with curves, so that explained the surprise that hit him. But he felt a warmth, too. Probably the result of doing a good deed. It couldn't be attraction. She wasn't his type.

He wasn't exactly sure why he needed to re-mind himself of that.

But he did.

Twice.

CHAPTER TWO

THEY WAITED UNTIL Seth and Harper left their reception at ten o'clock that night. Trent told Sabrina he would arrange for a flight crew while Sabrina said goodbye to her mom and Jake and Avery. Lighter now that she had a plan, she strode over to say her goodbyes, then Trent escorted her through the hot August night to the limo and they rode to the Park Avenue building housing her condo.

He exited the limo with her, but she shook her head. "No need to come with me. I won't be but a minute."

"A minute to pack?" He laughed. "I've seen how you dress. Everything coordinates. You're probably going to have a suitcase just for your shoes."

Offended because it sounded as if he thought her trite or spoiled, she strode to her building. "I'm not that picky." She wasn't picky.

She simply had a standard to uphold. If her mother had drilled that into her head once, she'd drilled it a thousand times.

You are a lady. Act like a lady. Dress like a lady. Speak like a lady.

With a quick push of her hand on the door, they entered the climate-controlled comfort of the lobby. Trent pulled a draft of frosty air into his lungs. She couldn't tell if he was happy for the cool air or uncomfortable about having to explain himself.

"I didn't say you were picky. I'm just saying you always look nice."

She worked to stifle a smile. It shouldn't please her that he thought she looked nice or that he cared that he'd insulted her.

But it had.

Puzzled, she led him to the elevator. She took out a key card to start it. "That's okay."

"Are we going to a penthouse?"

"No. Just an exclusive floor. Two condos. Half a floor each. I don't need a whole floor."

"Nice." He winced. "I still sometimes marvel at luxury."

She didn't ask him what he meant. She knew his beginnings. Her brother had told her Trent had blue-collar roots and had worked his way through university alongside Seth. Then he'd quit the job Seth had found for him to invest on his own. She admired him. It had taken guts to leave his convenient job and trust his genius. She should probably tell him that—

A funny feeling invaded her chest and brought her up short. She shook her head to clear it of the desire to figure out why she wanted to talk about that. Right now, she should be focused on throwing some clothes into a travel bag, driving to the airport, flying to France and facing Pierre—

Because she was pregnant. *Pregnant.* About to be a mom.

She pictured herself holding a tiny baby the way Avery had held Abby right after she was born. The sweet little thing would snuggle against her and, like Avery, she would marvel that she had created a life.

Warmth filled her, along with a sudden desire to cry. Happy tears. Now that she'd adjusted to it, being pregnant was like a dream come true. Her life was busy but established. She could take time off, create a nursery in her big condo, set playdates, take her baby for long walks in Central Park.

The elevator reached her floor. She stepped into the lobby with two doors. One to her condo. One to the condo of a nice, recently retired couple who traveled a lot. She had breakfast with them once a month when they were home, and if they ran into each other at the elevator, they chatted happily. They'd raised four kids and adored their three grandkids.

They'd be the perfect neighbors for a single mom.

She punched a code into her alarm to disable it, then pressed her key card to the lock and opened the door onto her pristine home.

Wide-plank hardwood floors ran through the open floorplan that included a white kitchen, formal dining space and living room with a long sofa in the center of three conversation areas.

She faced Ziggy with a smile. She'd already decided which room would be the nursery and that she could dismantle the third bedroom and turn it into a playroom.

"Okay. Now that you've nudged me, you can go. Thank you for the use of your jet. Honestly,

I'll be happy to compensate you for the flight crew and the fuel when I return."

His head tilted. "Oh, you think I'm just going to hand over my jet?"

"You're not?"

He laughed. "No. I'm coming with you. You're my best friend's little sister and you're pregnant. I'm not letting you fly across an ocean alone. What if you get sick? Or just faint? For at least the first trimester, I don't think it's wise to travel across an ocean alone."

She was surprised he even knew the word *trimester*, let alone that that could be a scary time for a woman, but she let that go in favor of her real concern. "I don't need help."

"Never said you did. My coming is more of a just-in-case thing. Just in case you get sick. Just in case you faint."

She wanted to argue, but she wanted to get to Paris more. It was night. She and Trent were both tired. They'd undoubtedly fall asleep for the entire seven-hour flight. When they woke in the morning, he'd be in a tux and she'd be in jeans and a shirt, suitably dressed to find Pierre.

Before Trent could buy proper clothes for a

morning in the city, she'd be at Pierre's apartment, telling him about the baby. He'd undoubtedly say he didn't want to be a dad and she'd say that was fine. She'd just thought he had a right to know he was about to be a father. Then she'd go back to the airport to fly home.

There was no point in arguing with Ziggy because she could make the timing work for her.

"Fine. Come to France with me, but all you'll be doing is sleeping on the jet. We won't even talk."

"I know the drill. I always fly at night."

"Great." Without another word, she walked to her bedroom to throw enough into an overnight bag to get her through a flight and a day in Paris.

When she returned to her main room a few minutes later, Ziggy stood by the wall of windows, staring at the twinkling Manhattan skyline. He'd removed his jacket and rolled his shirt sleeves to the elbows, revealing strong forearms peppered with black hair. He'd also taken off his bow tie and opened the top few buttons of his shirt. Now he was just a guy in black trousers and a white shirt. He *could* go with her to Pierre's condo.

It didn't matter. Even if he begged, she wouldn't take him to Pierre's. Surely, he could keep himself busy for a few hours in the most glamorous city in the world.

He took her overnight bag. "Ready?"

She slid the strap of her purse over her arm. "Ready."

She'd chosen jeans and a peach-colored T-shirt with brown wedge-heel sandals for the flight and had combed out her long hair. Because of the curls of the up-do, it flowed in gentle waves to her shoulders.

Ziggy's gaze traveled from her hair down her T-shirt and along the line of her jeans to her sandals. When his eyes met hers, a little jolt of electricity zapped her.

Now she knew what was going on. She *was* attracted to him. Sort of. The man *was* good-looking. But electricity? Sparks? She didn't believe in those. Never had.

Forcing herself to ignore the firestorm rolling across her nerve endings, she smiled her most professional smile at Ziggy and headed for the door. "Let's go."

"Sure."

They drove to a private airstrip and boarded the jet. The front of the cabin had four cream-colored leather seats. Behind those were two rear-facing blue leather recliners angled toward an enormous TV. It wasn't the kind of luxury she was accustomed to. Her family's biggest plane had two bedrooms, a kitchen and a formal dining room. But Ziggy's little jet was obviously expensive with plush carpeting, lush leathers. And it was convenient. With no unnecessary bells and whistles, it was almost cozy.

"All the seats recline." He pointed to a cabinet tucked behind the television. "Blankets are in there."

She tossed her bag into one of the empty chairs and got herself a blanket. "Great. I'm exhausted."

"Me, too."

But when she sat on one of the pale seats, he walked back to the blue ones in front of the TV. Glad he hadn't sat beside her—she didn't care to feel the crazy jolt of electricity she got when he was too close—she reclined the seat, snuggled into her blanket and almost instantly fell asleep.

She slept deeply and eventually dreamed she had twins who sometimes morphed into triplets, and every time she took them to the park, Ziggy followed her, walking a big, furry dog on a leash that sometimes got caught in the wheels of her babies' stroller.

The chaos of it jolted her heart. She woke with a start to discover they had landed in Paris, and decided her dream was an extension of Ziggy's following her around all day at the wedding. With a long drink of air to wake herself completely, she rose from her padded seat, grabbed her overnight bag and turned to go to the private area of the small aircraft.

Rushing to the door in the back, which she assumed was a bathroom, she didn't look right or left, not wanting to accidentally make eye contact with Ziggy. Or worse, wake him. The sooner she got out of here, the better her chances of leaving alone. All she needed to do was change her shirt, refresh her makeup and maybe take a minute to think about what she'd say to Pierre—

She opened the bathroom door and gasped.

Standing in the middle of the compact room, wrestling a shirt over his head was Ziggy— *Trent*.

A broad chest with well-defined muscles that led down to six-pack abs?

That was Trent. Adult. Sexy. And oh, so male. She'd never be able to think of him as her brother's college friend Ziggy again.

She spun away, her heart doing something that felt like a samba in her chest. "Sorry."

"No, wait. I'm done." He slid out of the room into the main cabin and tossed a duffel bag onto one of the empty seats. "Didn't want to be wearing a wrinkled tux around Paris."

"How'd you get an overnight bag?"

"There's always a go bag in my office. Had one of my assistants bring it to the plane while you were packing."

She worked not to glance down at his chest, now covered by a gray T-shirt. But the vision of his pecs and abs was firmly planted in her brain. "I didn't think you would be going to Pierre's apartment with me."

"I told you. You're my best friend's sister. I'm not going to let you go to some guy's house alone and tell him you're pregnant. God knows how he'll react."

"He's not going to hit me."

"You're damned right, he's not. I'm not going to let him."

The electricity she'd felt the night before came back with a vengeance as his dark eyes held hers. It took all the strength she could muster to keep her breath from stuttering when she said, "No. Really. You can't come with me. This is private."

"Oh."

The disappointed expression on his face knocked the electricity off her nerve endings but it tugged at her heart. This was a man who took his responsibilities seriously.

"Look. It's okay. He's going to say he doesn't want to be a dad. And I'm going to say *fine*, then fly back to New York and raise my child alone."

He gaped at her. "You don't want your baby to know his dad?"

"I do want my child to know *her* dad. But Pierre's not going to want to be a big part of her life. I won't be cruel. Pierre can visit anytime he's in New York. But I doubt that he will."

His forehead puckered. "He's not going to want his child?"

"Pierre's a narcissist. His parents had a marriage as bad as my mom and dad's and he vowed to make up for that by giving himself everything he'd wanted but didn't get as a child. I have to be practical. And honest. He told me he didn't want to have children and my being pregnant probably won't change that."

Trent shook his head. "You can't know that. You saw what happened to Jake. He about went crazy when Avery didn't want anything to do with him after she learned she was pregnant. Now he's so smitten with Abby it's almost funny. Then there's Seth. A confirmed bachelor until Harper walked into his life with Crystal."

"There was hope for Jake and Seth."

"No, there wasn't. Your dad had soured them both on relationships and made both wonder if they could be good dads…yet they pulled through."

"Neither one of them is a flighty artist like Pierre."

"But you loved him?"

"We had a relationship, based mostly on our common love of art. We also had the same kind of childhood. Pierre's not the kind of guy a smart woman falls in love with."

His eyes widened. "Wow."

"I'm just saying that Pierre and I had a lot in common and we had a great couple of years together. But we never wanted anything serious."

"Okay. I get that. But don't write him off."

She sighed. "Trent, I'm a planner. I teach other people how to look down the board and see the future. I've already played this all out in my head."

"I'll bet not all of it. You're going to want to get married someday. And when you do your baby's going to have a stepfather. *I* had a stepfather. He was a wonderful dad to my half brother and sister, the kids he had with my mom, but he never seemed to warm up to me. I was the boy my mom had with another guy. The one who came into the marriage. I wasn't blood."

Gobsmacked by the admission of something so personal and saddened for the lost little boy she pictured him to be, she said, "That's terrible."

He pulled in a breath. "Not really. The truth is he tried. I tried. We just never seemed to bond."

She stared at him. She'd always had the impression he'd come from one of those perfect, close-knit blue-collar families. "But now you get along?"

"Depends on what you mean by get along. When I left home, my mom, stepdad and half sister and brother became a tight little unit. I'd see it every time I came home for a holiday and feel more left out. When I became wealthy, I bought them a house and insulted my stepdad, who refused it and accused me of thinking I was better than they were now that I was rich." He shrugged. "So I kind of stay away."

She absolutely did not know what to say. Particularly since he'd just confirmed her decision to never marry. Even if her parents' marriage hadn't warned here off, she'd heard enough horror stories from her friends at private school, whose parents had gone through divorces. From middle school through high school she'd heard tales of wicked stepmothers and grouchy stepfathers. Having a child just guaranteed she'd never marry. She would not put her son or daughter through that.

He caught her gaze. "What I'm telling you is, if I had a choice between being raised by my real father or my stepfather, I know which one I'd choose."

Sabrina stared at him. He wasn't upset, more like resigned, but to Sabrina that made his situation all the sadder.

When she didn't respond, Trent turned her toward the small dressing room again. "Go. Change. Fluff out your hair. Do whatever it is women do to get ready. I'll be right here waiting for you."

She almost pivoted to face him again. He'd shifted gears from his own troubles to hers so easily it was as if his didn't matter.

With her problems being the ones in the forefront, she supposed they didn't. At least not now. At some point she'd circle back, ask him if he really was as okay as he sounded. But right now, she had to get dressed to tell Pierre he was about to be a dad.

She walked into the bathroom, splashed her

face and slipped into her clean clothes. Though she knew what she intended to say, there were three or four ways she could approach Pierre. Strong and confident. Soft and loving. Matter-of-fact. And even strictly professional, like a lawyer stating the facts.

All the options had merit. Even after a few minutes to think them through before she left the bathroom, none of them stood out.

Trent's staff had a limo waiting. The driver opened the back door for them, and she told him the address of Pierre's apartment. As they drove along the streets, she only got glimpses of the Eiffel Tower. But it didn't matter that she couldn't see the usual sights. She loved the everyday hustle and bustle of Paris. Brick and stone streets. Tourists studying maps or ogling buildings. And the scents. Croissants. Madeleines. Éclair. Wonderful crusty bread. And that rich, dark coffee she loved so much.

But she couldn't have coffee. She wouldn't drink coffee for nine months.

When they reached Pierre's apartment building in a residential section of the city, Trent followed her out of the limo.

She stopped him with a hand to his chest.

His very solid chest. She almost groaned at the whoosh of attraction that rolled through her. Instead, she shook off the woozy, fuzzy feeling and said, "This part is private."

"I'll tell you what. You let me walk you up to the door and see what kind of mood he's in. If he seems okay, I'll let you talk alone."

She wanted to argue. She wanted sexy, handsome, electricity-inspiring, nice guy Trent to disappear so she could tell Pierre he was about to be a dad.

Except, what if Trent was right? What if Pierre reacted badly? It wouldn't hurt to have tall, buff Trent in the loose gray T-shirt and nice-fitting jeans at her side.

"All right. You stay for a minute or two. Then the rest of the discussion is private."

He grinned. Her heart tumbled. How had she not noticed before how gorgeous he was with his unruly hair and seductive smile?

"Absolutely."

They entered the building and climbed the two flights of stairs to Pierre's apartment. It wasn't the best building in the world. But Pierre didn't make as much money as she did from her art. And that wasn't a lot. She lived on her salary from the nonprofit and an extremely generous trust fund.

Still, her leg muscles became rubbery when she remembered how angry he'd been when her art had outsold his at their last showing. Her steps faltered.

"You okay, there, Skippy?"

She pasted on a bright smile as she turned to face Trent, who was on the step below her. "Yes. Fine."

"If you want to turn and run, just let me know. I'm up for that, too."

Surprisingly, she laughed. For such a smart guy, with such a sad past and a serious way of making money, he had a great sense of humor.

They finally reached Pierre's floor and walked to the third door on the right. Forcing her fingers to stop shaking, she pressed the doorbell.

No answer.

After a few seconds she pressed again.

Trent sent her a confident smile and thumbs-up.

She hit the bell a third time. Pierre's door didn't open, but the one next to it did.

Pierre's short, dark-haired neighbor, Danielle, whom Sabrina had met a few times, came out of her apartment, smoking a cigarette. "He's not here."

Speaking French, Sabrina said, "Oh. Where is he?"

Danielle brought her cigarette to her lips, inhaled and blew a long stream of smoke. "He's at his house in Spain."

"Spain?" Confusion rippled through her. "He has a house in Spain?"

"He goes there at the end of every August. Pretty much spends the winter there."

Trent put his hands on her shoulders, reminding her of his presence to reassure her. "You wouldn't happen to have the address?"

Because he'd spoken English, Sabrina repeated the question in French. Danielle held up one finger. The universal symbol for "wait one minute."

She returned with the address written on a scrap of paper.

Trent said, "Thanks," took the paper, then turned Sabrina toward the steps again.

They walked down the thin stairway, her optimistic hope of telling Pierre and getting it over with, vanishing. Still, it wasn't like she had to wait forever. She just had to get to Spain.

When they reached the street, she took the slip of paper with the address from Trent's hand. "I can get a commercial flight. I don't want to bother you."

"It's no bother. Besides, I have a condo in Barcelona. We'll fly there, buy a change of clothes, eat a nice dinner and head to Pierre's tomorrow morning."

A weird kind of relief poured through Sabrina. Calm, cool and collected Trent had a plan.

Still, she didn't want to get accustomed to depending on anyone. Not ever. Her mom had been so dependent on her dad that she'd lost the biggest part of her life. Now that Sabrina was in Europe, away from her family's curiosity, she would have the privacy to do what she needed to do. She could go on without Trent.

"Thanks, but I'm fine."

"No, you're not. You're mad. The guy has a house in Spain that you clearly didn't know about. You dated him, probably told him everything about yourself but he had a house in

Spain and apparently spent lots of time there, yet he never thought to mention that. How much did you guys date anyway?"

She drew in a breath. She *was* mad. "We didn't *date* date. We spent weekends together, took trips, did exhibits together." She paused long enough to think through how to phrase her explanation. "Our homes were on two different continents. Our relationship was long distance. So there were stretches of time in the winter when we didn't see each other."

"Okay. I get it. That's how long-distance relationships are. You see each other when you can."

Once again, his answer relieved her. Most of her anger with Pierre melted away. But that didn't mean she needed Trent to fly her to Spain. "Thanks. When I tell Seth and Jake about being pregnant, I'll also tell them how much you helped me these past two days."

Trent's brows drew together as he frowned. "You do realize that what you're saying is that when Seth hears I brought you to France, I'll have to explain to my best friend why I dumped his little sister in Europe."

"It's not like that."

"That's exactly how a man would hear it. Especially when your brothers find out you didn't see Pierre in Paris. You saw him in Spain."

When she said nothing, he sighed. "Look, I'm offering a plane and some companionship. You could catch a cab to the airport and then wait two days before a seat opens up on a commercial flight. My jet's just a few miles away." He caught her hand. "And once we get to Barcelona I have friends, a condo, a club I like to go to. I might just ditch you."

She laughed. Again. He seemed to always say the right thing to make her feel better. He did have a plane. Here. Waiting. He also had somewhere for them to crash overnight. If he'd owned his condo in Barcelona for any length of time, he probably did have friends he'd want to go clubbing with.

And she'd have a few hours alone tonight for a bubble bath. She could chill and get her perspective back.

Because it *had* hit her all the wrong ways that Pierre had a home in Spain and in their *years* together he'd never mentioned it.

She needed some time to unwind and Trent was offering it.

How could that possibly go wrong?

"All right. Let's go."

CHAPTER THREE

TRENT CALLED HIS PILOT. Having an international cell phone, as Trent obviously did,
she was tempted to call her mom but decided
against it. When he finished his chat with his
pilot, they climbed into the limo and headed
to the airport. They landed on a private airstrip in Spain a few hours later, but it took
another hour to get from the rural airstrip to
Trent's condo.

When he opened the door for her and she
stepped inside, she gasped. The place was
amazing. Built in an old factory, the condo
retained the original brick walls, but they'd
been scrubbed to clean perfection. A row of
four tall, thin windows brought in light that
accented peach-colored club chairs across
from a modern gray burlap sofa. The coffee
table was a shiny wooden rectangle. Its open
middle would have been the perfect place to

stack magazines or books. But there were no magazines or books. Not in the open space of the table or strewn around. There wasn't a personal item anywhere.

"Let me guess. You don't come here often."

He tossed his keys on the long island of the spotless kitchen. Sturdy wood cabinets had been painted sage green. Shiny green, white and gray geometric-print tiles created the backsplash. Stainless-steel appliances completed the kitchen.

"No. I'm here all the time."

She glanced around. Even as particular as she was, she had magazines, books, pictures, scattered about.

"It's just all so…clean." Sanitary. As if he didn't have a personality. Or a family—

He had told her that he was distanced from his family.

The thought of not having pictures of Jake, Avery and Abby on her mantel or Seth, Harper and Crystal on the end table by her sofa squeezed her heart. The thought of not having her brothers and their families in her life or being in theirs almost brought tears to her eyes.

"I'm not one for having things lying around."

Okay. She'd give him that. But it had to be sad, difficult, having a mom but not being able to call her with questions or brothers and sisters-in-law to laugh with.

Before she could ask him about his family, he said, "Here's the plan. I'll contact my personal shopper. We'll have her send over some jeans, a few T-shirts and something nice to wear tonight so we can go out."

Not hardly. Her plan was for a soothing bubble bath. "*We* can go out?"

"For *dinner*. You do have to eat."

"Oh. Okay." She fought the urge to squeeze her eyes shut, dismayed with herself for jumping to conclusions. She was so uptight about Pierre that she kept assuming Trent was as bossy as her ex. She had to relax.

He picked up his phone, hit the screen three times and after a few seconds he said, "Claudine. I'm back in Barcelona. Unfortunately, it was an unexpected trip and I'll need clothes for at least another two days. Make it three."

He paused as Sabrina assumed the person on the other end of the call spoke. He laughed.

"Yes, everything, including something nice to wear out to dinner tonight."

He paused again, chuckling. He clearly liked his personal shopper.

A sliver of jealousy wound through her, surprising her. First, she had no claim on Trent—didn't want one. Second, the woman he spoke with was in his employ. She laughed with her employees all the time.

"I'm traveling with a friend. She'll need three days' worth of clothes and something pretty for dinner." He caught Sabrina's gaze and grinned devilishly. "Yes. You know my taste. Get her what one of my dates would usually wear."

Sabrina's eyes widened. She'd seen his dates in sparkly little red dresses that clung to their bodies but looked okay because they were wafer-thin. She, on the other hand, had boobs and hips.

"I can't wear what your girlfriends wear!"

Trent ignored her. "About a size eight."

Shocked that he'd hit her size on the head, she nonetheless stormed over to him. "I'm not wearing something you'd get for one of your girlfriends!"

He clicked off the call. "Oh, sorry. You said that two seconds too late."

"No, I didn't! You deliberately hung up, so I couldn't change what you'd told her!"

He ambled over to the sofa. "Is that so bad?"

"Yes! Your dates are thin as paper! I have curves."

"Exactly. Curves that you never show off. You'll look great."

"I don't think so."

"I do. Besides, wouldn't it be fun to be someone different for a night?"

She shook her head. "I don't do things like pretend to be someone different." It had taken her too long to become the perfect McCallan daughter to step out of character.

"You just made my point. You *don't* do things like this, things that are fun just for the sake of having fun. You need to loosen up a bit. If you don't like the outfit, it won't matter. We're in a city where no one knows you. You can toss the dress when we get home."

Seeing she wasn't changing his mind, she

marched to the Carrara marble island and grabbed his phone.

"What are you doing?"

"You think it's so fun to dress like someone else." She hit the redial button on his phone. "I'm calling your shopper and... Claudine? This is Sabrina McCallan. I'm Trent Sigmund's friend...the woman you're buying the dress for."

He sighed. "Seriously. I think you'll look great in something..."

Putting her hand over the phone she said, "Cheap? Sleazy?"

"Just a tad more sparkly."

She shook her head once, quickly, in disbelief. "Are you ashamed of me?"

He laughed. "Actually, I want to show you off."

Her breath stalled. He wanted to show her off—

She caught that thought before it could run away with itself. She was a McCallan. Her mother always said they had more dignity than to "show off." Still, she wasn't the one showing off. Trent wanted to show *her* off. Like someone who was important to him—

She'd never been important to anybody but her mom. She'd certainly never been important to a man. Her heart filled with warmth, but she fought it. She didn't need a man to show her off.

Still, one look at Trent's face and she knew she wasn't changing his mind. But the craziest idea popped into her head. "And what if I want to show *you* off?"

He shrugged. "Have at it." He took the phone from her hands. "Claudine. I'm going to put Sabrina back on the line. Get me whatever she says."

He handed the phone back to her.

She looked from the top of his curly black hair, down the chest and flat abs she remembered from the morning, to his feet.

"I think Armani. A charcoal-gray suit with a pale blue shirt... I want it to be such a pale blue that it's almost white...and a silver print tie."

He made a gagging noise.

She said, "Thanks, Claudine," then also asked for a curling iron and hair-dryer before she hung up the phone. "Now we'll see who likes dressing like someone else."

He shook his head. "I don't hate suits. I just don't wear them often." He grinned. "This is going to be a fun night."

She sighed. "You really need to get out more."

They bummed around for most of the afternoon, eating lunch, walking under the leafy canopy created by the trees lining the streets of Barcelona. She marveled at the simple beauty of the city. She'd never been to Spain before, let alone walked the streets of one of its fabulous cities. It was easy to see that Trent spent a lot of time here because he knew the best restaurants, said hello to passersby, was casually comfortable walking along.

When they returned to his condo around six, the purchases of Trent's personal shopper sat in two stacks of boxes and bags on the marble top of the kitchen island.

"Our clothes have arrived."

She strode over, running her hand along the first box. Pink-and-white-striped with a black bow, it reminded her of coming home from school and discovering her mom had been shopping that day. It usually meant her dad was traveling and dinner that night would be happy.

Sensation after sensation poured through her. Relief. Joy. Expectation.

"Want to look at what's inside or take everything to the spare bedroom and try things on?"

"I think I want a few minutes to myself with the red spandex dress." A few minutes to get her heart to settle down and to savor the good memories flitting through her brain. She hadn't had the horrid childhood her brothers had, but a river of caution and fear had run through their Upper East Side penthouse. Good memories had been few and far between. When they came, she enjoyed the feelings they brought with them.

She took the bags and boxes to the spare room and began sorting through to see what was inside. Two pair of jeans and a pair of shorts—Barcelona was a tad warm—undergarments, and the smallest dress in recorded history.

Her memories forgotten, she marched back to the kitchen, waving the little blue dress. "I can't wear this."

"Have you tried it on?"

She sighed.

He opened the suit box. "Don't forget I'm stuck with this."

"It's a suit. You've worn them before."

"And you've worn dresses before." He shook his head. "Come on. Let's just have some fun tonight."

The seriousness in his brown eyes reminded her that his childhood might not have been filled with fear, but it had been filled with loneliness. So he wanted to have some fun? Couldn't she, for once, forget her mom's voice in her head and do something silly to make someone else happy? Someone whose childhood might have been sadder than hers?

Not wanting him to realize she was capitulating because she felt an unexpected connection to him, she gruffly said, "All right. But I'm tossing this sparkly little thing when we return tonight."

He shrugged. "Fine by me."

She huffed back to the bedroom where she showered, fixed her hair, applied makeup. When she couldn't put it off any longer, she shimmied into the blue dress and stared at herself in the mirror.

It wasn't god-awful.

Okay. Seriously. She went to the gym three times a week so though she wasn't waiflike, she had a nice figure. And the dress—damn his hide—looked good. She wouldn't want to be wearing it walking around with her mother, but she was with a friend.

A male friend who wanted to see her in a tight dress.

She shook her head. This was Ziggy…

No. Actually, she was with Trent. Adult. Sexy. Trent.

She slid into the tall silver shoes the shopper had also bought. Trent had said she made distinctions that didn't matter? Maybe thinking of him as a different guy was one of them?

Maybe she should go back to thinking of him as Ziggy—Seth's friend, not hers—to end all this confusion?

Sabrina came out of her bedroom, and Trent's mouth fell open. He'd known she'd look good. He assumed Claudine had bought the blue dress to match with what Sabrina had instructed her to get for him—

But wow. Blue was her color and she was

born to wear the sparkly fabric that hugged her curves.

"I look like a hooker, Ziggy."

"No. You look like a woman who wants to have a fun night out on the town. And don't call me Ziggy." His voice softened with the familiarity he was feeling with her. "I like when you call me Trent."

He smiled at her and she weakly returned his smile. He couldn't imagine why a shift of names seemed to trouble her, so he turned in a half circle, showing off the Armani suit. "And how do I look?"

"Like a guy who forgot his tie."

He'd nixed the tie and had opened the top few buttons of his shirt in deference to the heat. But he also wasn't about to wear a suit dancing. And come hell or high water he was taking her dancing.

"Let's go."

She stayed right where she was. "If I'm going out in this, you're wearing your tie."

He relented. Not because she intimidated him but because he intended to get her on his side so that when he suggested dancing she'd happily agree. But he also had to acknowledge there was a certain boost a person got when wearing expensive clothes. He might like to fish. He might also be very at home in a small-town bar. But he was equally at home with power brokers.

Whether he liked admitting it, Sabrina was a sort of power broker. Smart and savvy, she could hold her own with the best of them. In a way, it was a coup that he'd gotten her to dress sexy.

Now he just had to come up with interesting dinner conversation that would win her over and put her in the mood to dance because if he was in Barcelona he was going to his favorite club.

But the second they were settled in one of Barcelona's beautiful restaurants and had ordered, she asked about his work.

"I buy stocks. I sell stocks. I buy bonds. I sell bonds. There's not much else to it."

"I know you think there's not much to what you do, but it's a skill. A gift." She looked at him over the salad the waiter sat in front of her. "Have you ever considered creating your own mutual fund?"

The horror of the thought almost made him choke. "Why would I do that?"

"I don't know. To contribute to society? To help other people?"

"Look, I have everything set up so that I do a reasonable amount of work and still have time for fun."

"I'm just saying you're the perfect person to create and manage a mutual fund."

She went on talking about business through the entire dinner. When dessert arrived, Trent felt four IQ points smarter, but not one iota relaxed.

He came to Barcelona to relax. She was ruining that.

"Do you always talk business?"

"No."

"Just with me, then?"

"It's the one thing we have in common." She shrugged. "My father always talked business at the dinner table with my brothers." She shrugged again. "It just seemed like the right thing to do."

Her past came into focus for Trent. "Let me get this straight. You talked business at the dinner table every night?"

"Not every night. My dad had business dinners some nights. When he was away, my mom would joke and play with us. But when my dad was around, we talked business."

"You think men only want to talk business?"

"Not just men. Women like to talk business, too."

"All the time?"

"Some of my most productive conversations are over lunch or dinner."

Knowing what he'd been told by Seth about their childhood and adding in this tidbit, even more of Sabrina's personality clicked for him. "Oh, honey."

"What?"

"We are so going dancing tonight."

He rose from the table, walked over and helped her with her chair. "Dancing?"

"I've seen you at charity balls. You love to dance."

And now that he thought about seeing her dancing, he realized he'd never seen her dancing with Pierre. Hell, he'd never seen Pierre.

"I do love to dance."

"Remember how much fun you had at the art show in Paris last year? The one where you could be Sally McMillan because your family isn't as recognizable in Europe as they are in Manhattan?"

Sabrina's heart stopped. One of her brothers *had* told him. "All right, who do I shake silly? Seth or Jake? That alter ego is a secret."

"Seth mentioned it and accidentally." He winced. "He was telling me how good your work is and how proud he was of you last year in Paris when you could be Sally because you knew you wouldn't be recognized."

Unexpected warmth filled her. It surprised her that her brother bragged about her, but it surprised her even more that Trent remembered something from a year ago. Some years Pierre forgot her birthday. He never remembered her showings, and even if he did remember to come, he wouldn't be able to recall what had happened an entire year later.

"I do remember how much fun I had that weekend." There had been an after-party where she'd danced and danced with Avery and Harper.

He smiled. "Then let's go dance."

She nodded as his argument sank in. Just as

in Paris the year before, no one in Barcelona would know her. Why not have fun the way she had in Paris? There'd be no one to tell her mom if she looked just the tiniest bit unlady-like in the shiny blue dress—

Except she didn't feel unladylike.

She felt—

Actually, she felt young. Carefree—

A woman who was going to have a baby felt carefree?

She couldn't explain it. But the reminder that she was a soon-to-be-mom about to go danc-ing didn't make her unhappy. If anything, new joy filled her.

So, yeah. She was going dancing.

CHAPTER FOUR

TRENT DIRECTED HER out of the restaurant and into the city. They walked a few blocks and Sabrina began to hear and feel the pounding beat of the music pouring out of a building a block away.

The sound lured her down the street and by the time they entered the club, she wanted to dance. Really dance. Not just get on the floor and gyrate. She wanted to move. She wanted to stop being tense and forget about telling Pierre. Tomorrow would be soon enough to worry about Pierre.

Partly because she felt different tonight. Sexier. She knew it was the dress.

A dress *Trent* wanted her to wear.

The weirdest heat raced up her spine.

He led her to a booth that had four people sitting in the semicircle bench seat. He motioned to the people, who gaped at her, wide-eyed with interest.

"Sabrina, this is Mateo and Luciana and Valentina and Samuel. My friends. Guys, this is Sabrina, my friend Seth's sister."

Two of them said, *"Hola."*

Two said, *"Buenas noches."*

Trent faced her. "I met Luciana and Valentina clubbing a few years back. Eventually, Mateo and Samuel joined the group."

With the music blaring around them, Sabrina could barely hear him, so she knew his friends hadn't. She couldn't explain the goofy looks on their faces as she and Trent slid onto the bench seat with them.

"You are enjoying Barcelona?" Mateo asked, his English made smooth and sexy by his accent.

She nodded. She was enjoying Barcelona. "We took a walk this afternoon, under the canopy of trees. The city is breathtaking."

Luciana nodded. "It's a great place. There's always somewhere to go, something to do."

Sabrina tried not to stare at her. She was American.

Valentina said, "New York is like that."

Luciana shrugged. "Sometimes. I like it here better."

"You like it here better because it's warmer," Trent said with a laugh. He whipped off his tie and jacket and tossed them onto the bench seat. Then he took Sabrina's hand and pulled her off the seat. "I promised Sabrina we would dance."

He guided her to the crowded dance floor. When they stopped, Sabrina said, "Your friends seemed surprised to see you here tonight."

"No, I'd called them and told them I was coming, bringing a friend. I think they're surprised that you're so beautiful."

"You don't date beautiful women?"

He laughed. "So this is a date?"

"No!"

With a sigh, he relented. "They are surprised that someone who is an obligation, the sister of a friend who needs some assistance, is beautiful."

It was the second time he'd called her beautiful. Offhand, casually, as if everyone knew. Or as if he couldn't stop noticing.

Her pulse sped up, and she stood there,

staring at him. He laughed at what must have been a very odd expression on her face, but the music called to her. She felt like dancing again and at this point dancing was a much better idea than finishing their conversation.

She closed her eyes, pulled in a deep breath and let the music take her. Even if Trent had friends in Barcelona, no one knew *her*. She could dance like an idiot and tomorrow it wouldn't be in the paper.

So she let herself go. Let the beat take her arms and legs, let all the tension of the past two days ripple away. One song turned into another. Trent caught her hands and she opened her eyes. Lights flashed. Music blared. He twirled her around once, twice and she laughed. The third song rolled in on the heels of song two. She noticed Trent's friends were on the dance floor, squeezing in a few feet away. People around them twisted and turned, bodies moving to the beat. Trent laughed and waved, a signal that she was wandering a bit too far away from him and she slid back.

Beside them, a couple danced close. Keeping her hand on her partner's shoulder, the woman circled him before she pressed herself up against him and kissed him. One of her legs grazed up his hip and back down.

Sabrina's eyebrows rose. The room got hot. Trent grabbed her hands again but this time he pulled her out of the crowd and over to their table.

"I think we could both use some water."

As she slid into the booth Sabrina said, "You don't have to drink water because I can't have a beer."

He slid in beside her. "Funny. I'd have never taken you for a beer girl."

"I'm not. Usually I like Scotch, but beer is good on a hot day, at a barbecue, or dancing."

"I'm having trouble picturing you at a barbecue."

"Avery and Jake own a house in the country...close to the small town where she grew up. Jake loves to barbecue."

A waitress came over and Trent ordered water for them both. When she returned with two crystal glasses filled with water, he drank his without complaint or qualm.

She took a long gulp of hers.

"I notice you don't seem uncomfortable in the dress."

She glanced down at the form-fitting, sparkling blue garment. The symbol of her freedom in Europe.

"You haven't tugged the hem down once."

She hadn't.

She caught his gaze.

"You have the legs for a short dress."

Electricity shimmied through her. She closed her eyes and shook her head. It was the weirdest thing to know someone for ten years and not really get to know them until forced to spend two entire days with them.

But that wasn't the weirdest of the feelings floating through her right now. She liked him. She might not believe sparks flying and blood shimmering were a good reason to date someone, but tonight she realized the feeling did exist.

He made her blood shimmer. When he looked at her, her chest tightened. Knowing he'd chosen this dress for her, maybe because he wanted to see her looking sexy, sent her heart rate off the charts.

She had honestly thought the poets were wrong. But here she was. Feeling things she never believed existed.

She bounced from the table. "Let's dance some more."

Let's get out on the dance floor, where we can't talk and I won't think about all these reactions that mean nothing.

She knew what love had gotten her mom. Heartbreak and fear. She didn't think she had any reason to fear Trent but giving in to these feelings would definitely cause heartbreak.

She slithered her way through the crowd to the dance floor. The pounding beat of the music urged her to move. Which was what she needed to do. Not to escape. Just not to think. Trent eased in beside her and before she knew it they were dancing beside the hot couple again.

The guy slid his hand up his girlfriend's neck and pulled her face toward him for an openmouthed kiss.

Sabrina watched, mesmerized. That would be how Trent would kiss. Sort of commanding with his hand hooking around her neck and pulling her close. But he'd also get right to the point with the openmouthed kiss.

She took a breath to clear her head of that thought, but as she did the music shifted again.

A ballad replaced the pulsing beat. Trent slid his hand around her waist and took her hand. Before she could think to say no, she was in his arms.

It was so different than anything she'd ever experienced that she almost froze. She caught herself before she missed a step in the dance, but she couldn't stop feeling. Even the fabric of the suit she'd chosen for him was soft, sensual. His hands were slightly calloused. And when she looked into his eyes, she all but melted.

He was intelligent, sexy and happy.

And she was in his arms. Close enough to feel the movements of his body, to savor the feeling of his shoulder under her palm—

She swallowed hard. They were in Spain because she was on her way to see the father of her child. A guy she didn't want to marry because she didn't believe in marriage. She didn't believe in love.

And Trent, like her brothers, needed love to heal from the wounds of his lonely childhood. He might not know it, but as much of a planner, analyzer as she was, it was clear as day to Sabrina. She'd witnessed what had happened with Jake and Seth. They floated through life, unhappy, until the right woman helped them face their pain and let it go. *That* was what Trent needed. And maybe there'd be a third unicorn woman out there who could care for him the way Avery and Harper had healed Jake and Seth.

She eased out of his arms.

She wasn't that woman. She didn't believe in these squiggly feelings. And even if they existed, her mom had felt them for her dad and she'd married him and been miserable, afraid, for forty years.

No one, no feeling, was worth forty years of misery.

Trent saw the happiness drain out of Sabrina's blue-gray eyes. For a good two minutes he'd watched her changing, watched her interest pique and her breath stutter, indicating she was every bit as attracted to him as he was to her.

Then she'd stopped, frozen, and whatever had popped into her brain, it sucked every bit of happiness out of their moment...

He fought the disappointment that surged through him. Not just for himself, for her. These feelings might be good, but they were ill-timed. She carried another man's child. And though she thought Pierre wouldn't want anything to do with their baby, he might surprise her. Trent couldn't do anything about their attraction until that situation was settled. For the baby's sake, he hoped Pierre would want to marry her.

But if he didn't…

That was a question for tomorrow. Tonight, no matter how much he was enjoying this, enjoying *her*, giving in to their unlikely attraction wasn't right.

He stepped back. "I guess we're ready to go home."

She nodded.

They said goodbye to his friends, who were still all smiles. He was sure they were confused about Sabrina. They knew him well enough to know she was more than just his friend's baby sister, but his normal dates were tall and thin with wild hair and mischief in their eyes. Sabrina was serious. Beautiful but serious.

His feelings for Sabrina confused him, too.

Which was another reason to back off.

The return trip to his condo was made in

total silence. In the lobby of his building, Sabrina gave him a sheepish smile.

"I'm just tired."

No. She'd figured all this out in her head, convinced herself they were wrong for each other and was back to her normal self.

Which was good. It *had to be good.* He didn't want to be the man responsible for keeping her baby from its father. Worse, he didn't want to be the fourth wheel in a relationship that should only have three: Sabrina, Pierre and their child. He'd already been the extra person in a family. He knew how painful and lonely it was.

They entered the elevator. The door swished closed and her perfume floated to him. He squeezed his eyes shut, trying to block it, but all that did was conjure visions of her dancing. Happily dancing. He hadn't seen her laughing at her brother's wedding, but she'd been happy tonight. Maybe because she'd been dancing with him?

He thanked God when the elevator doors opened. His thoughts were going in a very bad direction. Pride over showing a woman a good time was a normal male reaction. Especially a woman so beautiful. Especially a woman who had trusted him enough to wear the dress he'd chosen for her. And a woman who desperately needed a good time.

But that was all there could be to it.

They reached the door of his condo. He unlocked it and they stepped inside. She headed back to the extra room but pivoted to face him.

"Thank you."

Disarmed by her sincerity, he tossed his keys in the air and caught them one-handed. "For?"

"I could say stupid things like the dress or dinner or the fun time dancing, but that would be a cover. I needed to relax. You saw that. You helped me."

She said it as if no one had ever helped her before…

No. She said that as if no one had ever *seen* her before.

His heart contracted. No one had seen him most of his childhood. It had taken courage, genius and earning enough money to fund a small country before he'd felt seen, heard. Who would have thought a woman with two brothers who doted on her and a mother who thought the sun rose and set on her would feel alone?

He cleared his throat. "You're probably not going to believe this, but it really was my pleasure."

She smiled and caught his gaze with her big blue eyes. "Then maybe you should be thanking me."

He laughed because she expected him to. But a million thoughts raced through his brain. A million sensations bombarded his body. He hadn't felt this connection, this need, with anyone. Ever.

"I should." He paused for a breath. "Thank you. I really did have a great time." He wanted to kiss her so badly his chest ached with it. He wanted to show her she was beautiful and worthy of any man's attention. He longed for it with a desperation that surprised him.

But they weren't right for each other. And if they crossed a line and he hurt her, Seth would shake him silly...and he'd deserve it. But more than that, it would shift the focus of this trip. Maybe cause her to say no if Pierre wanted to expand their relationship because of their child.

He nudged his head in the direction of the hall, indicating she should go to her room. "Good night."

She nodded once. "Good night."

He tossed his jacket and tie to the kitchen island then sank into one of the two chairs in the living room. Using the remote hidden in the top of the wooden sofa table, he pressed a button that turned the huge mirror over the fireplace into a big-screen TV. He kept the volume down low enough not to disturb Sabrina and searched for something to watch.

It was going to be a long night.

Sabrina awakened the next morning feeling unexpectedly refreshed. She didn't know if it was too soon in her pregnancy for morning sickness, but so far, so good. No puking, no dizziness, no queasiness.

She showered and dressed in a pair of jeans and a pale blue T-shirt, but didn't slip her feet into shoes. Trent's condo was comfy. Homey. She padded barefoot to the main living area, telling herself she wasn't eager to see him. He was a fun guy. He had shown her a good time because that was who he was. She could have been as ugly as a muddy fence and he would have been a good host.

Because that was how she now saw him. Her host. Nothing more.

The night before, lying in bed, she'd convinced herself that everything between them was fine. There had been no awkward moment when she was sure he wanted to kiss her. Her pulse hadn't really skipped a beat when he looked at her, and her heart hadn't nosedived when she'd realized how good it felt to touch him. He was her brother's friend, doing her a favor.

That was even how he'd explained her to his friends.

All those things she'd *thought* she'd experienced had to have been one-sided. Otherwise, he would have kissed her.

Exactly.

She walked into the empty main area, hoping he stored bottled water somewhere. "Trent?"

The place was eerily quiet. Kind of like her condo before she raced out for work each morning. Empty. Echoing the sounds of her movements back to her.

She peered around the kitchen island, down the long row of sage-colored cabinets. "Trent?"

Well, she certainly wasn't going back to his bedroom to ask about something as simple as a bottle of water. She checked the refrigerator, found it empty and decided she'd grab her purse and go out to look for a shop that sold water…

Without the proper currency?

It was Monday. Surely, she could find a bank.

She was just about to return to her room to get her purse when the condo door opened. Trent stepped inside, carrying a tray with two paper cups, the kind that usually held coffee, and two bags.

"The two coffees are for me." He displayed a bag. "I have water in here." He nudged his chin toward the second bag. "And bagels and cream cheese in here." He set everything on the island. "Or, if you want, we can go out for breakfast."

"You had me at cream cheese."

"Good. Because I'm starving, and we'd wait at least twenty minutes for our food even if we went to one of the restaurants just down the street."

She rooted through the first bag and grabbed a water. After taking a long drink, she said, "Thanks. I didn't realize how thirsty I was."

"We danced a lot. I should have thought of that and had water in the fridge."

She might have relegated him to the role of host, but there was such a thing as being a demanding guest. A woman with proper manners would not do that.

"You don't have to wait on me. I'm fine."

"You're also my friend's little sister."

That reasoning was a good addition to her "host" theory for why he didn't want to act on the feelings that had pulsed between them the night before, and she pounced on it.

"Ah. Don't want to make Seth mad?"

He laughed as he walked around the center island, bent down and pulled out a toaster. "I've never been afraid of Seth."

She opened the bagels. "Really?"

He took two, split them and slipped them into the four-slot toaster. "Really. When we met, he was like a scared puppy. For all the lecturing your father had done, he hadn't taught Seth anything about the real world. Your brother knew how to do anything that involved money. He just didn't know how to get money."

Sabrina sat on one of the stools across the wide counter from Trent. "What does that mean?"

"Your brother's main source of income was an allowance. Anytime your dad withheld it, Seth went into a tailspin."

She leaned her elbows on the counter and her chin on her entwined fingers. "So what happened?"

"I was working as a waiter at a bistro and I got him a job." He shook his head. "I still remember him standing there, watching everybody, as if absorbing everything. Then he picked up an apron and a pad and pencil and he went to work."

"That simple?"

"Oh, he dropped trays and spilled a drink on a guy's head—"

She gasped. "Spilled a drink on a guy's head!"

"In fairness, a customer in a hurry bumped into his elbow."

"Oh, that's funny!"

"You're not supposed to get *funny* from the story. You're supposed to see how hard he tried." Trent shook his head. "No, I think what you're supposed to see is that your brother didn't think himself too good for work. He was eager to make his own way."

"That's why we didn't see him for two years?"

"You didn't see him because he was tired of being humiliated and embarrassed by your dad. He'd have gone to see you or your mom in a heartbeat, but he wanted no part of your dad."

"He hadn't seen Dad in years when he passed."

Trent's voice softened. "Your dad hurt him a lot."

"I get that."

"And what about you?"

"What about me?"

"How did you fare with your dad?"

The bagels popped out of the toaster. As Trent pulled them from the little slots, Sabrina found knives in a drawer beside the sink and opened the cream cheese.

"My dad thought I was adorable. My mom

capitalized on that. She taught me to be prim and proper." She took one of the bagels from Trent and began to slather it with cream cheese. "Very polite. Mannerly. It served me well."

Trent said, "Served you well?" before he took a bite of his bagel.

"As long as I never did anything wrong, he didn't yell at me or snipe at me or boss me around."

"Couldn't Seth and Jake have done that?"

"They weren't as cute."

He laughed. "I'm serious."

"So am I. I was an adorable child. Jake was all arms and legs and Seth didn't grow out of his baby weight until he was twenty. But also, they were guys. My dad wanted them to grow up tough and ruthless." She met his gaze. "As he was."

"And instead he turned them in the other direction."

"Jake was a maybe for a while. He might not have cheated or lied as our dad had but he was a hard-nosed businessman."

"Jake? The guy who melts every time Abby looks at him."

"It's why Avery didn't want to marry him. Why she was afraid to let him have a part in raising Abby. He didn't see anything but work, didn't care about anything but the McCallan legacy."

He finished the first half of his bagel. "Your family certainly has some tales."

"And we don't hide it. Hiding things was what my father did. So we're very open about our lives."

"Except Sally McMillan."

She snorted. "Sally's the exception. Otherwise, my work wouldn't be judged on its merit."

He grabbed the second half of his bagel. "I get it."

"Do you?"

"Well, as much as I can. I didn't grow up surrounded by maids and drivers. We didn't have to worry about the people who worked for us carrying gossip out to the street."

"There was more to it than that." She slowly spread cream cheese across the second half of her bagel. "My dad had a temper. We all just tried to stay out of his way."

He took a sip of coffee. "I'm sorry. I didn't

mean to diminish what happened in your penthouse."

She shrugged. "You didn't. We all ended up fine. Even my mother."

"That's good."

She smiled and nodded but looking into his dark eyes, she remembered that everything from his not-so-happy family hadn't worked out. Oh, he had money and brains—genius—but he was alone.

"Anyway, the point of all of this was to explain that your brother and I grew very close while living together and working together. It started off as me and my friend Clark, then Clark brought in Seth. Then after a year or so Harper moved next door and Clark fell for her like a ton of bricks and spent all his spare time at her apartment. Then it was just me and Seth hanging out, working together, going to school. I taught Seth some street stuff. He taught me about investing and saving. And we both landed on our feet. I think of him as more than a friend. I think of him as a brother."

She considered that for a few seconds. "You think you owe him."

He bobbed his head in agreement. "Yes."

"He thinks he owes you and Clark."

"He owes Clark because none of us would have had a place to live if Clark hadn't come directly from the Midwest with enough money for a month's rent and a security deposit."

"But he owes you for the street smarts."

He laughed. "And he paid me back by teaching me things—and introducing me to the right people—after getting all three of us a job in an investment firm right out of university."

"Why didn't you throw in with Seth and Clark when they started their own investment firm?"

"They were conservative." He laughed devilishly. "I wanted to roll the dice."

"Lucky for you."

"Yes." He took another drink of coffee. "So what time do we leave for the ranch?"

She glanced down at her jeans and shirt. "I'm ready now."

He spread his hands accommodatingly. "So am I."

"Let's clean this up and we can head out."

"I'll clean up. You go get your things."

She rounded the island and pushed his hands

aside when he reached for the bag of bagels. "Don't be silly. I can clean up."

He watched her make short order of tying the twist tie around the bagels and storing them in a drawer as he tucked the extra water into the fridge and wet a paper towel to wipe off the countertop.

Understanding wobbled through him. It was as if she went out of her way to let people know she wasn't pampered or spoiled. Seth and Jake hadn't had to do that because stories of their father's abuse had rippled into Manhattan's folklore. But Sabrina had been the adorable little girl. The one their father had doted on.

He supposed that was a good enough reason for her not to want to be thought of as spoiled—though compared to Seth and Jake she had been.

When everything was clean, she turned to go back to the extra room, but he stopped her. "Let's get all of our stuff and that way we can drive to the airstrip from Pierre's."

He didn't want to mention that when they got to Pierre's and she told the Frenchman about their baby, Pierre might want her to stay, and this way she'd have all her things. Trent was nothing more than a guy doing a favor for the sister of a friend. It would be good for her and Pierre to talk this out, maybe even needing a few days together to get through all of it, maybe deciding they wanted to make a commitment for the sake of their child.

But that didn't mean he had to like it.

In fact, he absolutely hated it. She rarely danced with Pierre. She never talked about Pierre making her happy.

And he was delivering Sabrina and her baby right to his door.

That was beginning to rankle.

CHAPTER FIVE

TRENT WAITED FOR her to get her things from the extra room and laughed when she came out lugging a suitcase bulging at the seams.

"We should stop and get you another bag. Or you could just leave some of the clothes behind with the blue sparkly dress."

She pretended great interest in searching through her purse. "Actually, I packed the blue dress."

That brought him up short. "Really?"

She met his gaze. "It grew on me."

Her eyes flickered the tiniest bit. A person who hadn't known what to look for would have missed it. He almost teased her about wanting the dress as a memento of a good time but stopped himself. He liked the idea of something he'd bought her hanging in her closet. He couldn't have her, but it was nice that they'd made a connection. Nice that she wanted to keep something he'd bought her.

He made a quick call to the doorman and when they stepped out onto the street, his shiny black Jaguar awaited them. The doorman opened the passenger-side door. She got in and Trent rounded the hood to get behind the wheel.

"I still say you should start a mutual fund."

Ah. On a long drive, the safest thing to talk about was business.

Punching the address of Pierre's house into the GPS, he said, "Not a chance."

"Maybe volunteer to be a mentor at my non-profit."

He laughed.

"Maybe give just one lecture."

He almost said an automatic, "No," until he realized that getting involved with her business would keep them connected, keep him in her life. The scramble of his pulse at just the thought told him it was a bad idea. He was taking her to the father of her child, the man she should at least consider letting into her life, for her baby's sake. There was no place for him in that equation.

He pulled the car onto the street. "I'm a professional hider. Normal people don't know who I am. Bankers do. Investors do. But I can go to a coffee shop or restaurant without being recognized. I like it that way."

She said, "Humph," and settled back on her seat, but he could see the wheels of her brain were turning.

"You're not going to change my mind."

"You're so sure."

Keeping his attention on the road, he said, "Yep." He paused for a second then said, "Don't you like being Sally McMillan, getting away from your life?"

She cut him a look.

"That's my life all the time. Private. Secure. I can do anything I want—as long as I don't break the law—and no one cares."

The GPS took them out of Barcelona and onto a long stretch of road that wound through the country. The day was warm, the sun bright. Rays hit the leaves and grass and seemed to shimmer around them.

"Mind if I put the car's top down?"

She ran her hand down her loose hair. "Sure.

It's not like I have a hairdo. Even if it tangles, I can brush it out. So I'm game."

He pulled off the road and lowered the top. In a few minutes they were cruising again, taking the advice of his GPS, with the wind in their hair. The noise of the air swirling around them precluded conversation, but there was something poetic about the silence. He liked peace and privacy. He loved the beauty of Spain and he felt like he was sharing that with Sabrina, a woman who seemed to use business—even the business of her art—so she didn't really have to experience life.

Shaking his head at the stupidity of his thoughts—he was neither a poet nor a philosopher—he cleared his head and focused on enjoying the drive. A little over an hour later, the GPS took them through a series of turns that led to their destination.

As he navigated a long lane framed on each side by wood fences that created a corral on both sides of the roadway, he watched Sabrina take it all in. Cattle, barns and outbuildings, all under the dome of a matchless blue sky.

He stopped in front of a pale brown stucco house and said nothing as she stared at the huge two-story structure. An etched-glass door, trimmed in dark brown wood with two glass globe lights standing sentinel, held her attention for at least a minute before she glanced over at him.

"Maybe he just rents the house?"

Trent shrugged. "Maybe." He hopped out of the car and eased around to the passenger side. Sabrina still hadn't moved. Heat shimmered around them in the stagnant air. The cattle were too far away to hear. If there was farm machinery working, the sounds of it also didn't reach the house. The dwelling had probably been located here for exactly that reason. To protect it from the sights, sounds and smells of the ranch.

It seemed Pierre was a tad craftier than everyone had given him credit for.

Trent opened the door. Sabrina delicately stepped out, but Trent suddenly envisioned her in the same jeans and T-shirt except wearing boots and a cowboy hat rather than sandals with her wild hair flowing around her. Would it even occur to her that she could fit here? Would it even occur to her that the prim and proper way her mom had raised her was

to please a dad who had been dead for years...
that she could be herself?

She passed her hand through her hair as if
just remembering it had been tossed by the
wind for over an hour. But rather than reach
for a brush or comb, she glanced around again.
Then shook her head and pointed at the steps
leading to a porch with a dark brown railing.

"Let's go."

His heart sank. It was almost as if she'd seen
what he'd seen. With her hair slightly messed
and in blue jeans, she belonged here.

Would Pierre see that, too? Would the father of her baby see her in his home and realize she could fit?

Did Sabrina want Pierre to see her in his
home and recognize that she belonged here...
with him?

Sabrina took a silent breath, hoping to un-
scramble the confusion in her brain as she led
Trent up the steps of Pierre's house. She saw
dollar signs everywhere. The pristine grounds,
the older home that had clearly been remodeled; the sheer expanse of land around her

told her this was no winter retreat. This was a working ranch.

Still, she pasted a smile on her face before she rang the doorbell. As she waited for Pierre, she wished Trent wasn't with her because she had the oddest sense she was going to lambaste her ex for lying. Even if it was a lie by omission.

It so wasn't her. She didn't lambaste anybody. She stood up for her clients. She also stood her ground with her clients when they didn't like her advice. She could be tough, determined.

She simply didn't get into fights. She didn't lambaste people. She rarely even raised her voice. She let her facts and figures stand on their merit.

She didn't need to lambaste anybody.

She rang the bell again and looked around the ranch one more time.

A ranch might not be her style of living, but for heaven's sake, if Pierre owned this, he'd been seriously downplaying his net worth to her, getting her to pay his airfare to the US when he visited, letting her subtly pick up every check in every restaurant.

The insult of it resurrected an indignation she couldn't quash, as outrage over his dodging expenses sent a crackle of energy through her veins.

This time when she rang the bell, she hit it hard and let her finger rest on the button. The sound was so loud they could hear it on the porch.

"You might want to ease up on the bell, Skippy."

"He's not going to ignore me."

The door jerked open. A middle-aged woman with dark hair and huge dark eyes gaped at her as she rattled off something in Spanish.

Sabrina glanced at Trent who said, "She wants to know why you're holding on to the bell."

Sabrina yanked her finger away.

"Tell her I'm here to see Pierre."

He said something that Sabrina couldn't translate but which ended with Pierre.

The woman answered. Trent turned to Sabrina with a sigh. "He's not here."

Sabrina spun to face him. "What!"

"Pierre's not here. She's a maid just finishing her weekly work, about to go home for the day."

The maid said something else.

Trent smiled and nodded. *"Sí."*

Sabrina said, *"Sí?"*

"She asked if we'd like to come in for a cold drink."

Oh, she'd like to go in, all right. She'd like a bit of a look at Pierre's "winter" house to see what else he was hiding from her.

"Sí. I'd like to come in."

The maid held open the door. Trent motioned for Sabrina to enter first. She stepped into a glamorous entryway with a huge chandelier and shiny black-and-white tiles arranged like a checkerboard.

The maid directed them to a room with the same flooring as the foyer. The far wall was a bank of windows that provided a stunning view of grass and trees growing against the backdrop of the mountains. A piano sat in front of the windows with a tall table, about bar height, against the wall by the door, but otherwise the room was empty.

Trent said, "Wow. I wonder how much it would take to get him to sell this place."

"Shut up."

He winced. "Sorry. I know you thought he was a struggling artist. And he might be." He brightened. "He could have inherited this ranch and be really grateful to his dead relative because he's not making enough from his art to support himself."

"Don't defend him."

The maid returned with a pitcher of something that looked like lemonade and two glasses.

Trent thanked her, then added another line that caused the dark-haired woman to nod and scamper away.

"What did you say to her?"

"I asked her to give us a few minutes."

"For what? To see how wealthy my struggling artist ex-boyfriend really is?"

"More like to let all this sink in."

"You mean the fact that he lied?"

He sniffed a laugh. "I thought you'd say something like he withheld information."

"You thought I'd defend him?"

"I thought you'd split hairs. It seems to be how you comfort yourself."

The maid returned, talking a mile a minute as she pointed at her phone.

Trent said, "Something's come up. She has to go. She said she shouldn't have let us in at all, but she recognized you from the picture on the piano and knew you must be a friend of Pierre's."

"The picture on the piano?" Sabrina walked over and found an eight-by-ten picture of herself—a candid shot, not something professional—framed in wood among a group of pictures. "Oh."

The simplicity of it made her breath catch.

"Don't go all mushy on the guy."

Her gaze snapped up. "All mushy?" She laughed. "No. Oh, no. I'm just a bit confused. Pierre's passionate, but not sentimental." She pointed at the group of pictures of people who had to be friends. "All this doesn't add up. He had money but never picked up a check."

"Because he was a cheapskate?" Trent suggested sarcastically.

She shook her head. "I think it was more about him maintaining an image. I thought he was a starving artist. Maybe he wanted to perpetuate that impression?"

"And now you're back to splitting hairs." He quickly downed his lemonade then angled his chin at the maid, who stood wringing her hands. "Let's go."

Sabrina headed toward the door, but the maid stopped them. Her dark eyes softened. She said something that ended in Italy.

Trent nodded and ushered Sabrina through the foyer and out the door. It wasn't until they were in the car that Sabrina said, "He's in Italy, right?"

"Yes."

"The man does travel."

Trent laughed as he started the engine. "She said if we go to his website, we'll see the address of the gallery where he has his showing."

She let all this new information about Pierre flow through her. Now that she'd wrangled her temper into submission, she reminded herself that they'd had a passionate but surface relationship. She could also understand why he'd withheld things. Neither had committed fully to the relationship. That was their deal.

"I don't blame you if you're angry."

"Actually, I'm not angry. I'm thinking. The

bottom line is, Pierre hadn't told me everything about his life, even though I'd told him everything about mine."

He cut her the side eye. "Which is why you have a right to be mad."

"No. I told him everything about myself to explain why I didn't want anything from him but a nice, passionate fling. Part of the way he'd complied was to not tell me anything about himself."

He groaned. "Oh, my God. You've gone from splitting hairs to defending him."

"No. I'm understanding him."

Trent shook his head. "You are the strangest woman."

"No, I'm not. Lots of women are logical."

"Haven't you ever just wanted to let go?"

Had he missed the part where she'd kept her finger on Pierre's doorbell?

She glanced at him. With his attention fixed on the road, she could take a minute to study his perfect nose, high cheekbones, curly black hair. She had wanted to let go the night before. She had wanted to kiss Trent and just let whatever happened happen.

But being with someone like him was the opposite of how she'd spent her entire life. Protecting herself.

Trent Sigmund would entertain her, amuse her, treat her like a princess, make love like a desperate man one minute and a smitten man the next…and he'd disappear as quickly and easily as he'd entered her life. Because he didn't commit. The man didn't even have a picture in his Barcelona condo. And then she'd be hurt.

She had no feelings of pain because of Pierre. Sure, she'd been lonely. And seeing his extravagant home in Spain—and working ranch that probably netted him a boatload of cash every year—had been enough of a shock to boil her blood.

But she wasn't hurt.

Pierre did not have the power to hurt her because she'd kept her emotions out of their fling.

"Did you know my mom was crazy-mad in love with my dad?"

He stole a quick peek at her. "No."

"My dad blew into my mom's life like a hurricane. She wasn't wealthy, but she was beautiful, and she knew it. She'd thought that her beauty had gotten her the love of a wealthy, sophisticated man, and she felt like she'd won the lottery because he hadn't just been swept away by her. She'd been swept away by him. He spoiled her, ravaged her, bought her things, was good to her family."

"And when they got married, all that went away?"

"Yes. Except she still loved him."

"How could she love him after all the things he did to your brothers?"

She shrugged. "By the time he started bullying my brothers, her love had faded. But he threatened to use his money and power to take us away from her if she filed for divorce. She knew the only way she could protect us would be to stay married to him."

He shook his head. "Wow."

"That's what love does to people. That's the real result of letting go. And I will never—never *ever*—set myself up for any of that. Maybe, in a way, Pierre just proved himself to be like my dad, too."

Trent's eyes snapped to hers. "Did he hurt you?"

"No, but he did prove he can't be honest about money."

CHAPTER SIX

TRENT STARED AT her for a few seconds. They'd begun this journey with him not exactly rooting for Pierre, but at least hoping that she would let Pierre into their child's life. He still wanted her baby to know his dad, but he didn't agree that Pierre couldn't be honest about money. He thought the guy was a cheapskate.

But hearing her story about her parents, knowing she'd lived a difficult life when her dad was around, he suddenly understood why she wore stuffy suits and conservative cocktail dresses.

In a way, he also understood why the Sally McMillan pseudonym worked so well for her.

She was so afraid of life and love, afraid of getting close to someone, so afraid of getting hurt, that she downplayed her assets, dated a guy she knew she'd never fall for and wouldn't even consider being herself because she was protecting herself.

And he didn't blame her. He protected himself, too. His public appearances were few and far between—all so he could remain anonymous and be able to go to a restaurant or coffee shop without being mobbed.

He drove down the lane and turned to the right to make the return trip to the airstrip. "At least we packed and don't have to stop in Barcelona for our things."

She smiled.

His heart clenched. She might not be hurt but something was wrong.

"I just wanted to get this over with."

He nodded at her cell phone. "Google his website. Let's see where he is in Italy. We'll hop on the plane and be there in a few hours. Once you've spoken to him, I know a fabulous out-of-the-way restaurant. Family-owned. Mamma Isabella is still the main cook."

She started typing into her cell phone. "I love Italian food."

And he could share that with her. She couldn't drink, so he couldn't open a whole new world of wines to her. But she could eat.

Mamma Isabella's spaghetti Bolognese was to-die-for. He paused. Mamma's spaghetti might be awe-inspiring but just the thought of her lasagna made his mouth water.

They'd eat outside on the restaurant patio so they could hear the night sounds and smell the earthy scents of the Tuscan air as the sun went down and the world quieted.

Then, tomorrow, if she'd let him, he'd fly her to Venice to show her the beauty of that city and take her for a ride on a gondola.

Excitement filled his chest. He'd taken a few of his female friends to Italy, Barcelona, Paris, but he'd never had this primal urge to experience one of those cities with them. Sabrina was hungry for experiences. Hungry for someone to see her. And he saw her. He knew who she was, what she wanted—

If she hadn't been in the car with him, he would have cursed. There would be nothing between himself and Sabrina. Even if Sponge-Pierre CheapPants flat-out rejected her and their child, she didn't want a man in her life. For good reason. And he had his fears about being a stepfather, hurting her child the way his stepdad had unwittingly hurt him. It was crazy to long to show her the world he'd discovered because they couldn't share it.

"I've got his website."

His chest hollowed out. The thought of showing his world to her was the first personal excitement he'd felt in decades. And he'd talked himself out of it.

He took a quiet breath. Worked to put some excitement in his voice when he said, "Good."

"Clicking upcoming events."

He waited as her phone processed.

She frowned. "His announcement about Italy is in red."

He glanced over. "Red?"

Her fingers moved over her phone. "Oh. Italy is canceled."

"Oh."

Then why did he leave Spain?

Trent didn't ask the question aloud. Sabrina's emotions had been on enough of a roller coaster for one morning. But all kinds of things popped into his head. Like Pierre's Paris neighbor might have called him and warned him Sabrina was coming so he could hide from her.

The thought of it set his blood on fire. She

might not have wanted anything permanent or serious with Pierre, but from everything Trent had seen of the guy, he was a louse.

"Here's something interesting."

He sure as hell hoped it explained Pierre's behavior, or when they finally did catch up with him, Trent wasn't sure he could be responsible for what he said or did to him.

"What?"

"There's a personal note from him explaining that his manager had overbooked him."

One of Trent's eyebrows rose. The guy was just full of excuses.

"There's an event in Ireland he does every year. A charity thing. It's not the same week every year so when his manager presented him with the opportunity for the Italy exhibit, he agreed, not knowing it coincided with the fund-raiser in Ireland. Something he's committed to supporting."

Trent tried not to give the guy credit for a soft heart toward the charity, but fairness forced him to.

Sabrina stopped reading.

He waited for her to say something. When thirty seconds went by with no response, he said, "So, Skippy, does this mean we're going to Ireland?"

"I guess."

Her lackluster response could have meant she was disappointed, or tired, or simply tired of chasing after SpongePierre.

"You know, you could send him an email."

She gaped at him. "To let him know he's going to be a father?"

"Yeah. I guess that is a little cold."

"He might not be the best person in the world, but I was raised better."

She certainly was.

She retrieved the information about the Ireland exhibit and he instructed her to forward it to his pilot.

It was dark before they landed at a private airstrip near Dublin. His assistant had contacted a rental car agency and a representative waited with the keys to a shiny black SUV. The man grinned and Trent smiled. His staff had been instructed to tip the man handsomely. Obviously, they'd listened.

After the copilot loaded their bags into the back of the SUV, Sabrina and Trent climbed in. They buckled up, Trent spoke the address of the hotel into his phone's GPS and the screen lit up with directions.

Sabrina gaped at the message. "We're an hour away from the hotel?"

He turned on the ignition and started the engine. "At least."

"Why do you use airstrips so far out of a city?"

He chuckled at the impatience in her voice. "Well, your brother Seth taught me that's the easiest way to sneak into town."

She crossed her arms on her chest, settled into her seat. "Sounds like Seth."

"Your brother Jake taught me that if you get a limo and a driver, you'll have an extra hour to work in the car as you are driven to the hotel."

"That's Jake."

"But I think it's the best way to see a country."

She turned to him, her face scrunched in confusion.

"Your entire family is on fast time. That's the part of the rat race I opted out of when I decided to go into business for myself."

"This has nothing to do with the rat race." She pointed outside her window. "It's dark."

She said the words as if he was daft.

He laughed. "Just think of the fun we'll have seeing Ireland on our return trip."

The moon suddenly appeared from behind a cloud. It didn't exactly bathe the area in golden light, but there was enough to see hills and trees.

The GPS gave him directions and they headed toward Dublin. When they finally arrived at their hotel, they stumbled in, exhausted and ready for bed. They registered for the rooms his assistant had booked, and each went their separate ways, agreeing to meet in the lobby for breakfast.

After a good night's sleep, he showered, dressed and took the elevator downstairs where a freshly scrubbed Sabrina—her long yellow hair in a ponytail—awaited him.

A hostess led them to a table and when she left, Sabrina said, "The event tonight is formal."

"Not exactly a blue sparkly dress affair?"

She busied herself unfolding her napkin. "No."

Okay. No joking around this morning. Not that he blamed her. This time they weren't popping into Pierre's apartment, arriving unannounced at his ranch or going to a city where he "might" have a showing. They'd seen the website. Tonight at eight o'clock, Pierre would be at a renovated castle in the country-side. He would show his art, donors would bid on the pieces, and the money would go to the charity sponsoring the event.

She would see him tonight.

So no jokes. No intrusion into her thoughts. This was her thing, not his. In fact, a smart escort might bow out, give her some time alone.

They ate their eggs and pancakes in near silence. When breakfast was finished, they left the restaurant, but he paused in the lobby. "I actually have a little bit of work to do this morning."

Hope lit her blue eyes. "You do?"

"Yes. But don't worry. I'll find a place to get a tux."

She glanced around the elegant lobby. "I should probably get a gown."

She looked so forlorn, so tired of chasing Pierre, he knew he had to do something to lift her mood. "I don't suppose you'd let me pick it out."

She laughed, then squeezed her eyes shut. "I think I better stick to my own style tonight."

He tucked his hands into his jeans pockets. "Okay."

She smiled slightly. He couldn't tell if she was relieved to be getting rid of him or glad to have gown-shopping to keep her occupied, so she didn't have to worry about what she'd say to Pierre.

"Okay."

Either way it didn't matter. She had things to do and despite the fact that he had to escort her to the showing that night, he didn't want to be in the way.

He especially didn't want to sway any of her decisions about Pierre. Though part of him questioned his judgment on that. He liked her. He was ridiculously attracted to her, and the side of him that went after goals like a bulldog desperately wanted to be let loose.

It wasn't like him to want something so badly and not go after it.

* * *

Sabrina returned to her room, did a little research on the internet and found the perfect boutique to purchase a gown for that evening.

She called for a taxi and was at the shop in forty minutes. Small, exclusive, the boutique had everything from the latest jeans to designer gowns. She had no desire to impress Pierre. She actually wanted to blend into the crowd, so she could ask for ten minutes alone with him, tell him he was about to be a dad, watch his face lose all its color and then tell him he could have as much or as little to do with his child as he decided.

She could probably do all that in jeans, but she didn't want to call any more attention to herself than she would draw when she asked for some private time with the star of the show.

Which meant she should probably wear pale blue. Most blondes did. It would be the best color to wear for blending.

A sales clerk came over, her smile light and pleasant. "How can I help you?"

"I need a gown." She winced. "For tonight."

"How close are you to a size?"

"Very. In the United States I wear an eight.

No alterations required. I'm not sure what that translates to here."

The clerk waggled her fingers to direct Sabrina to a small sitting area in front of a dressing room. "I have three things that are absolutely stunning. You wait right here, and I'll bring them for you to try."

She returned five minutes later carrying the expected pale blue gown. Behind her was a younger woman holding a pink gown and a bright red one.

A sparkly red one.

She laughed. Then pressed her fingers to her lips.

The clerk said, "Is everything okay?"

"Yes. Fine. The red dress just reminded me of a friend of mine."

"We should try it first, then."

"No. We should try the blue one. It's the one I'll probably get. No sense wasting time."

The clerk helped her into the dressing room where she hung the pretty blue gown on a hook. Sabrina stepped out of her jeans and T-shirt and slid into the dress.

She felt nothing. She'd been wearing pale blue to please her dad since she was two and her hair had darkened from baby white to a soft yellow.

Still, looking like herself wasn't a bad thing. It was just a thing—

Or maybe she could try on the pink one?

She slipped out of the dressing room to tell the clerk she'd like to try the pink one. The clerk wasn't around but the pink and red gowns she'd chosen for Sabrina hung on a rack a discreet distance from the door. She could scoot over and grab another dress to try.

At the rack, she reached for the pink one but removing it from the hook revealed the sparkly red one.

It was so fun. So pretty. So open and honest. The construction indicated it would cling to her curves…but so what? In a few months she'd have a basketball for a stomach. Maybe she should take advantage of this opportunity to show off her still-flat tummy?

She slid the pink dress back to the hook and took the red one into the dressing room.

She swore she heard the sparkly dress laugh at her.

Okay. All right. It wasn't her usual style, but

she'd had such fun in the blue clingy dress in Barcelona.

Was she saying Trent was right?

Hell, if she knew. She was pregnant and about to tell the father of her child he was going to be a dad. If she wanted to be a little—idiosyncratic—then she should let herself. She'd been in four countries in three days. If she wanted to wear red sparkles, so be it.

She slid the dress off the hanger and discovered it was backless. Devilishness slid through her. She stepped into the dress, slipping her arms into the long sleeves and then straightening the slim portion on her shoulders before facing the mirror.

Wow.

She grabbed her ponytail and twisted it into a knot at the top of her head, accenting her long neck, but also showing off her entire back.

Her entire back.

She looked like somebody else. Not like the little dress-up doll she'd been as a child. Not like the pulled-together businesswoman. Not like Sabrina McCallan, society woman, benefactor. Or even like Sabrina McCallan, aunt to

Abby and Crystal and soon-to-be aunt to Jake and Avery's next baby.

She looked like…

She hesitated to say it…

But…

She looked like herself. Maybe for the first time ever, her real self. The self she knew she was deep down inside.

Studying her reflection, she swallowed hard.

Not because she was confused. Because she was overwhelmed. Had she really let other people rule her life so much that she wasn't herself?

Hadn't ever been herself?

She imagined walking up to Trent at the lobby of their elegant hotel, the red dress molded to her curves, her hair a waterfall of yellow curls caught so high that they barely reached her shoulders.

Would he be mesmerized?

Would he whistle?

She laughed. The jokester would whistle, and her face would redden, but she'd laugh. He always made her laugh. That was why she liked—

She snatched the dress off her shoulders,

slid the sleeves down her arms and stepped out of the dress.

That was ridiculous.

She didn't like him. Well, she liked him as Seth's friend. And yes, she was noticing for the first time that he was so much more than what she'd thought. But the timing was all wrong.

And even if it wasn't…

Ultimately, he would hurt her or she would hurt him. He needed a wife like Avery or Harper. He needed a woman who didn't mistrust and fear emotions. He'd never said it. But she'd seen the magic the right woman worked with Jake and Seth and she was no one's right woman.

She took a breath, told herself to stop thinking about Trent as she put the red dress on the hanger again, shimmied her T-shirt over her head, wiggled into her jeans and stepped out of the dressing room.

The clerk raced in to meet her. "I'm so sorry! We got a customer, then another, then another."

Sabrina smiled. "It's okay."

"I see you tried the red one!"

"Yes, and it's lovely." Perfect. "But I'm going with the blue one."

She would have called herself a coward, but there was no point. In a way she was chickening out. But for good reason. This event wasn't about her and Trent. It was about her telling Pierre about their baby. She'd be crazy to muddy the waters with other emotions. Stupid emotions. Emotions she did not like or trust. Emotions she wasn't even sure she knew how to express or handle. She'd already shocked herself enough with seeing her real self in the red dress. She couldn't be throwing those other emotions into the mix.

In fact, for fifty cents she'd tell Trent to go home.

She *should* tell Trent to go home. She knew the place of the event, had something to wear, could get dinner on her own…and then face Pierre and catch a commercial flight home.

That was exactly what she should do.

Exactly what she *would* do.

She found a quick lunch and spent a few minutes idly walking the streets of Dublin, in love with the quaint shops and deciding to come back after she had her baby so she could visit a pub. She had a friend or two who would be happy to travel to Ireland with her, and she'd also decided to have a full-time nanny…that is if her mom didn't insist on coming along to help her with the baby. Her mom had turned out to be the most amazing grandmother. She wouldn't hesitate to allow her the opportunity to be a huge part of her baby's life.

Walking back to the hotel, seeing the shops, watching the tourists, picking out residents from the tourists, she suddenly understood why Trent liked to travel an hour through the countryside from the private airstrips he chose.

She would bet he was probably having a high time, walking Dublin's streets—that is if he wasn't in a tavern, convincing the locals he knew as much about soccer as they did.

The thought made her laugh, then pinched her chest with a longing so sharp she almost stopped walking. She would love to tour this city with him.

But she couldn't give him what he needed, and she wouldn't cheat him. What would have happened to her brothers if they'd settled for a woman who didn't know how to love?

She quickened her steps, got herself to the hotel and out of the temptation to see herself with Trent as quickly as she could. In her room she picked up her phone and tapped the contacts button to call him to let him out of his commitment to her, but also to get herself back to normal.

He didn't answer. She left a detailed message, explaining she had her gown, she'd eaten lunch, she was ready to face Pierre...

And he could fly back to New York now, rather than tagging along. She would check into commercial flights the very second she hung up from calling him. There wasn't even a reason to call her back.

She bit her lower lip. "And thanks. Not only do I appreciate the use of your plane, but you were a big help."

Well, that just sounded cold and impersonal.

"What I mean is I had fun in Barcelona. You helped me keep my cool over Pierre's ranch. And I did see Spain and some of Ireland—even though it was dark."

She sighed. That just shifted it over to too personal.

She said a quick goodbye and hung up before she dropped her phone to a convenient chair and headed to the big bathroom of her luxury suite. She ran water in the tub and used some of the bubble bath available for guests. Twenty minutes later, relaxed and crinkly from the time in the water, she got out and wrapped herself in the big fluffy robe also provided by the hotel.

Tired, she sat on the bed, then lay down—just for a minute—then immediately fell asleep.

She woke with a start two hours later. Gasping, she realized she just barely had enough time to arrange for a car to pick her up before she showered and dressed.

She wasn't even sure she'd have time for dinner.

Which was fine. She'd had a big lunch. She raced into the shower to wash her hair and would have simply raced through getting dressed, except she picked up the curling iron to do her hair and remembered Barcelona.

Dancing and almost kissing.

She ignored the wave of attraction that tried to steal her breath, plugged in the curling iron and walked to the hotel room phone to call the concierge to see about getting a car to drive her to Pierre's event.

With those arrangements made, she returned

to the bathroom and spent the next forty minutes styling her long, thick hair. She applied makeup, refusing to think of Barcelona, then stepped into the pretty blue gown.

But when she slid into the silver shoes bought by Claudine, Trent's personal shopper, she couldn't help thinking of him. About dancing. About watching the other couple kiss and wondering what it would be like to kiss Trent that way. About longing for it. About knowing—with a woman's intuition that she'd always thought only a myth—that he'd wanted to kiss her, touch her, when they'd returned to his condo.

Her breath stalled as a confusing mix of yearning and self-doubt assaulted her. She told herself to stop thinking about things that couldn't be. But when she walked by her phone, still sitting on the Queen Anne chair, she looked down and saw there was a message.

Her heart sped up, but she forced it to slow down again. She'd called him and told him to go home. The polite thing to do would be to call her to say goodbye.

Might as well listen to it and get it over with.

She pressed the button to retrieve the message, but it wasn't Trent. It was her mom.

"Sweetie, where are you? I stopped by your apartment with cinnamon rolls the other morning and you weren't there. I figured you'd left for work early but when I went by today you weren't there again. I almost had your superintendent let me in to see if you were alive…but you know me. I'm not one to panic or butt in."

Sabrina laughed. Her mom panicked and butted in all the time.

"Call me."

She would. As soon as she talked to Pierre, the return trip to the hotel after the charity event would give her time to call her mom, when everything was settled.

Happy with her plan, she left her room, her essentials in the little silver evening bag Trent's shopper had bought for her.

Trent.

Sexy, smart, considerate Trent.

She checked her phone. He hadn't called her.

He had to have gotten her message. Maybe he didn't think a response was necessary? In fact, in part of her babbling message hadn't she told him it wasn't necessary for him to call back?

Wrestling with disappointment that she didn't want to feel, she headed for the elevator, got in and rode to the lobby. She turned to walk to the concierge desk but stopped dead in her tracks. There, chatting with the exuberant concierge was Trent.

Dressed in a tux.

His curly hair wasn't its usual wild and free. It had been cut and styled in a short arrangement that accented his sharp features, especially his dark eyes. He was cute, adorable, sexy, with his long, curly locks. With his short hair, he was devastating.

He looked up. Their eyes met and his were not happy.

CHAPTER SEVEN

SEEING SABRINA, TRENT sucked in a breath. She was so perfect it almost hurt to look at her. But he was also furious.

Call him and tell him to go home? Forget what he'd told her about Seth skinning him alive for dumping his baby sister in Europe?

His temper flashed at just the thought.

She sauntered over, the filmy skirt of her gown rippling. "Did you not get my message?"

His anger threatened to spill over. He took a second to stifle it before he said, "I am not dumping Seth's baby sister in Europe."

Though right at that moment she didn't look like anyone's baby sister. The skirt of the gown might have been full and flowing but the top cupped her breasts and lifted them like an invitation. Her long, silky curls kissed her shoulders.

He shook his head. Yelling at her or drooling over her wouldn't solve anything. "Your car is here."

She held his gaze with cautious blue eyes. "Okay."

He motioned to the door. "Let's go."

They headed to the revolving door. She started to speak but he cut her off. "Don't tell me I'm not coming or that you don't need me or that I can go home. I started this and I'm seeing it through."

Early-evening traffic filled the street, providing a cacophony of noise and confusion. Sabrina didn't argue when Trent climbed into the black sedan with her. The driver closed the car door before walking to the front and sliding behind the steering wheel.

They said nothing for the first ten minutes. He waited for an apology or even for her to start an innocuous conversation to get them beyond his anger. When she said nothing, the dam of his emotions broke.

"It kills me how you cannot understand that if I left you, Seth would be furious."

"Seth will be on his honeymoon."

He groaned. Always practical Sabrina would be the death of him. "He'll hear about this sometime and when he does all he'll see is that you were in a life crisis and I abandoned you."

"This isn't a crisis. It's a situation."

He gaped at her. "Does everything have to be so logical for you? Can you just once get mad? That man, Pierre—" he said the name with a disdain that rolled off his tongue like fiery darts "—didn't deserve the time he got with you."

No man really deserved her. She was soft and sweet. But hardened by a childhood with a father who expected her to be a perfect little doll. The man she finally let loose with, was honest with, had to be someone special. Someone who would see she deserved to be treated with kindness and love.

Not merely passion.

And right now the feelings he had for her were nothing but passion. He was angry, but she was gorgeous, sexy. He could picture every move of making love to her. He could almost see her reactions. Hear her coos and sighs of delight.

He scrubbed his hand across his mouth. It sounded as if he wanted to be that man. And he had to admit he liked the heat that raced through his veins when he thought about keeping her in his life, but that was wrong. He was a man made to be single, to enjoy life, to forge his own path. She was pregnant with another man's child, a woman who would need stability to bring order to her world right now.

And if both of those weren't enough, she was the sister of his best friend, which made her strictly hands-off.

"I know Pierre better than you do. I know how to approach this."

The reminder that she had to be hands-off stemmed his anger and shut down any fantasy he might have of being the man who brought love to her life. "Yes. Of course. I'm sorry. I shouldn't be butting in."

Obviously puzzled by his quick change of heart, she studied him for a few seconds before she said, "I get it. You're like Seth. You want to fix things."

He snorted. "Don't confuse me with your brother. I'm not a fixer. Seth is."

"He's like that from spending a lifetime trying to make everything run smoothly when our dad got home."

"I understand."

* * *

Sabrina did, too. She always had. But something about saying it out loud, after seeing herself in the red dress and realizing she was only now finding herself, caused puzzle pieces to shift and scatter and then come back together as a totally different picture.

That life of scrambling to please her dad was over.

Not just because he was gone, but because her brothers had moved on. Both were married now, creating their own families.

Her mother had moved on. She was the happiest grandmother on the planet.

And with the birth of her baby, *she* would move on.

She glanced out the window. Halfway between daylight and dark, the world shimmered with an eerie glow, but she could see trees and grass, a world outside the city on the way to a castle.

A castle. She was going to a castle.

A man on a bike rode the side of the narrow country road. Lights began to flicker on in houses.

The simplicity of it stalled her breath, made her smile. "Ireland is pretty."

"Just figuring that out?"

She was figuring out a lot of things. Like it had taken years and maybe even a pregnancy for her to shake off the sense that she still had to please everyone.

The inside of the car quieted. Lost in thought, she didn't say a word. Trent didn't, either. Finally, the driver turned onto a long lane and after a few minutes pulled the sedan up to the castle.

As she stepped out of the car, she saw that the sky had totally darkened. A blanket of stars twinkled overhead. She leaned back to see them fully, then breathed in a long draught of air. Like the cloudless sky, her brain had cleared. The weirdness of the time since her dad's death found meaning. She'd wanted to move on but had so many habits ingrained in her behavior that she'd felt like she was treading water. Now that she understood that, bits of her life finally made sense.

"Ready?"

Except him.

Trent's being in her life made no sense. She

wasn't even sure what he was doing here. Though he'd certainly stirred things up. Made her think. Maybe even helped her to realize it was okay to move on.

She glanced at him. With his shorter, slicked-back hair, his cheekbones were sharp, his dark eyes dominant, crystal-clear and focused. His full lips created a mouth just made for kissing.

The thought should have baffled her, but she'd thought about kissing him before, had wanted him to kiss her…still wanted him to kiss her. That was even more confusing than trying to figure out how to tell Pierre he was about to be a dad.

She straightened her spine. That was exactly why Trent was a distraction. A woman shouldn't be thinking about a new man until she totally settled things with the last one—

She stopped her thoughts. She couldn't lie to herself or let herself make up excuses. The truth of why she needed to stay away from Trent had nothing to do with Pierre. She'd never been attracted to a man this way before and it scared her. The hunger inched itself into her thoughts at the worst possible times. And it was wrong. Attracted to him or not, she couldn't give him what he needed.

She had to ignore everything she felt for him. "Let's go."

They walked up a cobblestone path to a huge gray stone castle. Spotlights in the grass surrounding the building highlighted turrets and stained glass. Two men in tuxedos stood by the enormous wooden doors. Obviously original, they'd been sanded and treated with a dark stain.

As Sabrina and Trent approached the doors, the two young men yanked on the handles and pulled them back, revealing the huge, well-lit foyer where men and women milled about, holding champagne flutes as they examined the paintings on view.

Sabrina gasped. "I can see why he didn't want to miss this."

Trent shrugged. "As parties go, it's a seven." He pointed to a huge picture of Pierre over a fireplace. "Or, if that's a picture of Pierre, maybe he likes the fact that these people seem to adore him."

She sniffed. The crowd parted, and Pierre

walked out of a side room and into the group like a movie star making a grand entrance.

Trent shook his head. "If he just got here, we have to give him time to mingle."

"We? Don't think you're coming with me."

"You already told me that. But you should know that if I think things are getting ugly, I'll be in there so fast he won't get his next word out."

He took a champagne flute from a passing waiter. "Could you get a glass of water for the lady? And put it in a flute." As the waiter walked away, Trent said, "No point making it look obvious that you're not drinking."

She calmly said, "Thanks," but her insides churned. She'd dated Pierre for years, yet she hadn't known about his ranch, hadn't known about an event he did every year. When she saw the pretty girls approaching him, hanging on his every word, she knew why. He'd liked her, but he loved this attention.

That registered as a simple fact. She wasn't jealous or angry. She was finally seeing that she hadn't been paying much attention to who he really was—because he wasn't right for her and she'd always known it. She'd dated him for fun and he'd probably spent time with her for the same reason. Now she had to tell him he was going to be a father and she knew he'd be upset or angry. Or both. Their relationship had been free and easy, and creating a child was about as serious as it gets.

The waiter returned with her water. She and Trent walked around, looking at Pierre's paintings. She found the area in which she could bid on one of them or donate to the charity and she gave the assistant the appropriate information for a sizeable gift.

"Sabrina. How lovely to see you!"

At the sound of Pierre's voice, she turned—

Just in time to see Trent stiffen.

"Pierre, this is Trent Sigmund. Trent, this is Pierre." Tall, thin, wiry Pierre. Good-looking enough with his round eyes and black hair, but not really anything special. Not devastating like Trent.

Refusing to think that through, she caught Pierre's arm. "Is there somewhere you and I can talk privately?"

He glanced at Trent, clearly believing him to be her boyfriend or new lover. "Privately?"

Seeing no reason to disabuse him of a notion

about something that was none of his business, she said, "Yes. I have something I need to tell you."

Though Pierre seemed unhappy about it, he pointed at the door to a room on the left. "Of course."

She went in ahead of him and he closed the door behind him. "What is this important thing you have to tell me?" He sauntered over and caught her upper arms, his smile warm and intimate. "If you're looking to get back together, I'm open to a discussion."

Revulsion rippled through her. Even assuming she had a new boyfriend, Pierre made a pass at her?

She stepped away from him. "No. It's not that kind of something." She took a breath. She was so far over him that sharing a child with him took on a new meaning. Something more objective. Something businesslike. "I'm pregnant."

His mouth fell open. "What?"

"I'm pregnant."

He stepped back. "I hope you're not here thinking we'll get married."

"No." She almost laughed at his narcissism,

as if she'd gotten pregnant to trap him into marriage. Lord, the thought of a lifetime with him almost made her shudder.

"Oh, really? Why else would you fly across an ocean so soon after your brother's wedding?"

It took a few seconds to figure out what he meant. "Oh, you think I got all starry-eyed at the wedding?" She shook her head. "No."

"You'd better not." He walked even farther away from her. "Because we'd talked this through."

Her patience with him hit a wall. "You know what? Sometimes you behave like a real child. I've always known you filtered everything through the lens of your own benefit, but this is ridiculous." She stepped into his personal space. "I don't want anything from you. In fact, if you'd tell me you wanted nothing to do with our child I'd go home a happy woman. I'm perfectly capable of raising this baby alone… No. I *will* raise him or her alone. But for the baby's sake, you might want to be involved in her life. If not…" She shrugged. "I'll give her your name when she's eighteen and what happens from there will be up to you."

She turned and began walking out the door but spun around to face him again. "You should probably also grow up before your child turns eighteen." She almost turned to walk away again, but said, "And get my picture off your piano."

Pierre's faced whitened. "What? How did you know about…?"

"Nice ranch, by the way. I should bill you for about a billion dollars' worth of lunches and dinners…not to mention hotel rooms and airfare."

She pivoted and walked to the door, which she was sure Pierre had closed. Yet, here it was, open. She strode through, not bothering to close it for Pierre.

Her shoulders straightened. The long breath of air she took filled her lungs with something that felt a lot like freedom. Or empowerment.

She had been young when she began dating Pierre. She might have been smart, but she'd been sheltered, inexperienced…and maybe confused by her parents' relationship. She forgave herself for missing all the obvious signs that the guy was nothing but an egotistical spoiled brat. But she wasn't confused now. She felt strong, capable, intelligent—

Like a woman who was right where she was supposed to be, doing exactly what she was supposed to be doing.

Hiding along the side of the door, Trent had watched it all. Unable to bear the agony of waiting, he'd slid to the entry of the room where she and Pierre talked, turned the doorknob and jumped out of the way when the door opened on its own.

He'd heard every word and when she'd started to walk out, he'd slipped a few feet to the left and then gotten himself into the middle of the crowd looking at Pierre's paintings.

He'd stopped just in time to see her stride out, take a long breath and then grin.

She hadn't bested Pierre. There was no win or lose in this situation. There was only control and she had kept it. With or without Pierre, she intended to raise this baby properly.

She spotted Trent standing in the middle of the exhibit room and walked over.

Her blue eyes shone. Her grin…yes, a grin on sophisticated Sabrina McCallan…lit her face.

"Well, that was easy."

"I saw. Do you think he's going to want to have anything to do with your little boy or girl?"

"I don't know. But if he does, I'll set some ground rules, making him see the baby in New York, maybe even in my condo while I'm present until I determine what kind of influence he intends to have. And if he doesn't…" She shrugged.

Trent laughed. "You'll give your child his name and address when he turns eighteen and let it be up to the kid if he wants to know his dad." He laughed again. "That was perfect."

"No, that was fair."

He wanted to kiss her so bad he had a hard time controlling himself. Sabrina McCallan was strong, knew her mind, had been right about Pierre all along and would make a fantastic mother.

She glanced around at the people milling about the exhibit. "I'm ready to go."

"I'll have the valet tell your driver. But first—" He slid his hands to her waist and yanked her to him, planting his lips on hers out of sheer excitement.

But when his mouth pressed against the softness of hers, longing shivered through him, his common sense disappeared and instinct took over.

Kissing her was like his first taste of champagne, sweet and bubbly, but with a bite. That bite was his own need sliding through his blood. The scary thing was only a tiny bit of it was sexual. The need was more about the joy of sharing and connecting. To a man who made it a point to keep a safe distance to protect himself, tumbling head-first into an emotional connection was as sharp, as urgent, as anything sex could offer.

And also as frightening.

He tried to pull back, to save himself, to remind himself of everything at risk, but she caught his face and kept him right where he was, deepening the kiss by opening her mouth beneath his.

CHAPTER EIGHT

SABRINA GAVE HERSELF over to the kiss, curiosity urging her on. But when she realized what was happening, that this was Trent, the guy she'd wanted to kiss with a ferocity that confused her, she melted. Every cell in her body felt alive as if she'd awakened from a long sleep and was seeing morning for the first time.

She swiped her tongue along his, reveling in the sensations that spiraled through her as she linked the great, humble, determined, sexy guy she was getting to know to the man kissing her. The muscular shoulders beneath her trembling hands stiffened. Jumbled thoughts vied for attention.

She was just out of a bad relationship.

She was pregnant with *that* man's child.

Her parents had shown her the worst example of love imaginable. She'd seen firsthand what happened when two people who shouldn't have even become involved got married. Love was a plethora of intense emotions that caused people to make bad decisions. What she was feeling for Trent wasn't merely out of character; it was also out of control. Like speeding down a highway in a car so big your feet can't reach the brakes. Much like what her mother had described she'd felt for her father.

Trent made another move to pull back, but hesitated. His warm lips moved ever so slowly, ever so gently, across hers again, building an ache in her chest. She wanted this so badly. Wanted *him* so badly. But this wasn't just about her, her fears, her troubles. She also knew *his* history, knew he needed a woman who was softer, more in touch with the emotions currently making her heart feel like it would explode.

She couldn't be the woman he needed, and to get involved with him would only muddy the waters of his life.

She pulled away, pretending great interest in straightening her skirt.

After a few seconds he said, "That was a surprise."

She wouldn't look at him. She might have finished the kiss, but he'd started it. How could he call his own action a surprise—?

Unless his feelings for her had overwhelmed him, as well?

It didn't matter. He needed—no, he *deserved*—more than she could give. She suddenly wondered about her competency as a mom. Emotionally deficient as she was, would she also be unable to give her child everything she needed?

She took a breath. Straightened her shoulders. Even in a bad situation, her mother had been the best mother in the world. She'd taught Sabrina everything she needed to know to assure that her child always felt loved, cherished, protected.

Trent watched her distance herself. He could have almost scripted the conversation in her head. She had a baby to care for. She didn't need a distraction.

That was fine. He knew all that, too. And he

wasn't here to find a new lover. He was here
to support her.

"I was proud of you back there."

She finished her imaginary straightening
of her skirt. "Thanks. I felt empowered. Not
doing what everybody would have told me I
should do but doing what I knew was right."

Ah. And there it was. The reason she'd
kissed him back, lured him into a deeper kiss
when he would have ended it so much sooner.
Standing up to Pierre, making a clear decision
about her life, about her baby's life, had given
her courage or confidence.

Which she would need to get through a pregnancy and raise a child.

A man who messed with that process would
be as much of a narcissist as Pierre.

And Trent wasn't. He was a man in a weird
situation. Attracted to a woman with a child
on the way, when he was a guy who knew
the realities, the difficulties, of step-parenting.
Even people who tried often failed, and some
of his scars from being left out still pinched
sometimes. For the first seven years of his
life, he and his mom had nearly been insepa-

rable. Then she'd remarried and he'd gotten left behind.

The truth he'd always avoided crawled out from a far corner of his brain. If his mom hadn't remarried, he and his mom would have remained the team they'd become when his father died. Because she'd remarried, the older Trent had gotten, the more he'd understood that he couldn't begrudge his mom companionship, or more children, so he'd been the collateral damage.

He'd always looked at his genius, his success, as fate's way of making that up to him, and he accepted that and didn't reach for more. Actually, he'd never wanted more—hadn't wanted to test the waters of real love. He was okay with knowing he was an outsider, a loner.

Until that kiss.

He'd say he was a good kisser or she was a good kisser, except he knew the explanation wasn't quite that simple. It was more that *they* were a great combination.

But they were the wrong two people. Or maybe it was an accident that they clicked. Because they could not follow through on this. Not with her pregnant and him very aware of the troubles, the heartache, when a man couldn't accept a stepchild.

Their situation sucked. If she wasn't pregnant, they'd date, and he could analyze if their clicking meant something or not. As it was, his decision had to be made immediately. They couldn't test the waters. They couldn't play around and see if anything would become of what they felt.

He had to decide right now if he was willing to risk hurting her, risk her child's happiness. Or worse, risk the possibility that he could take away the opportunity of her and her child forming a great bond that would last a lifetime.

And right now the answer had to be no.

In the back of the car, returning to the hotel in Dublin, awkwardness ruled. A man could make up his mind that doing something was wrong, but that didn't mean a kiss won't haunt him.

After the strained first half hour of the forty-minute drive, his brain scurried to think of a neutral topic of conversation and all he could come up with was, "So how would one go about starting a mutual fund?"

His face hurt from holding back a wince. What was he doing? He had no intention of starting a mutual fund.

She faced him. "I'd probably let an investment firm do the heavy lifting on the setup." She shrugged. "Your name would carry the fund and you'd have to pick the stocks or bonds your company supported."

He held her gaze. She was dangerously smart and very easy with her knowledge. Even the way she phrased things spoke of casual understanding of finances. He saw her father's influence. All those dinners where he'd grilled her brothers, she'd been paying attention.

"But I know you don't want to start one. You were tired of the silence in the car, groped for something to talk about and picked a topic you knew I couldn't resist."

In some ways he loved her honesty. In others, he wanted to run from it.

"I also noticed that you didn't ask about volunteering to mentor or lecture at my nonprofit. It's okay. I know that mentoring or lecturing for me would mean we'd see each other again. And I don't think either one of us wants that. Since Seth's wedding, we've been feeling something for each other." She sneaked a peek at him. "And we don't want to."

He'd been so gobsmacked over her admission that she'd felt something for him that he almost didn't hear the "And we don't want to."

When it sank in, he took a breath. He understood why he didn't want to. He didn't want to hurt her, to hurt Seth's little sister, or to hurt the relationship she would form with her child.

But all this time he'd leaned on the fact that she didn't believe in love to keep himself from taking what he wanted.

Now she was telling him she felt things for him? Making him want to forget all the reasons he had to stay away from her?

She might be brilliant about finances, but she knew nothing about shutting down an attraction. Because what she'd just said rippled through him like a challenge.

"Yeah. I'm not a very good risk for a ready-made family."

She shook her head. "Or maybe you are, and you just haven't found the right woman? Someone soft and sweet."

He would have snorted at that, except he remembered the way she'd kissed him. So hungry. So greedy. And he couldn't believe she didn't see herself as the right woman. But her expectant tone of voice, as if the strategist in her knew exactly what he needed, told him that she didn't see herself in that role.

Even after their powerful kiss should have clued her in that she really could be.

He rolled all that around in his mind and the only conclusion that made sense was that this might have been the first time she'd ever kissed someone she had genuine feelings for.

It humbled him.

And scared the hell out of him.

But if they talked about this any more, she'd be in his arms again that night and this time he wouldn't pull away.

"So I'd contact an investment firm—"

She laughed. "Don't want to talk about the attraction, huh?"

"Hell, no. *My best friend's baby sister?* We might be having some feelings but we both know they're wrong. I'm not a good candidate to be anybody's stepdad and if I hurt you, I'd lose my best friend. Now that you've talked to Pierre, we have, at best, twenty-four more hours together. Eight of those we'll be sleeping in separate rooms at the hotel. We can sleep on the plane or work on the plane. And once my driver drops you off at your condo in New York, we'll only see each other at parties Seth hosts. No one has to know any of this."

"So we've got what? Twenty more minutes of painful silence?"

"Not counting the hour-and-twenty-minute drive to the airstrip tomorrow morning." He shook his head. "Couldn't we talk about favorite TV shows?"

"I don't watch television."

"Good. Then I'll tell you about all my favorite TV shows."

He babbled on for ten minutes about everything from half-hour comedies to full-blown sagas on platforms he paid to access. To keep her brain from going in directions she didn't want to go, she paid close attention.

"So there are knights?"

"Yes."

"But it's present day?"

"Well, sort of. It's an alternate reality."

"Interesting."

"It is! It's interesting to think about how different life would be if one little thing in history hadn't happened or had happened differently."

Their gazes caught.

She didn't have to wonder why he'd stopped talking or where his thoughts had jumped because hers had tumbled in the same direction. What might have happened if they'd met under different circumstances? If she wasn't pregnant. If he wasn't someone who needed a woman more like Avery or Harper. Someone who knew how to love.

Because she didn't. Up until a few days ago, she hadn't even believed love existed.

Holding his gaze, she quietly said, "I wasn't talking about the show. I was talking about the fact that you're so enamored with television."

"Ah."

The car pulled up to the hotel. Trent opened the door, got out and extended his hand to help her.

"My brain likes to be busy. What does it hurt if it's rummaging around deciphering an industry or enjoying an alternate reality?"

She stepped out onto the sidewalk. "I guess none."

Still holding her hand, he led her into the

well-lit lobby. Working to keep their attention on something that made no difference in either of their lives, he appeared to have forgotten he still held her hand.

But Sabrina hadn't. No one had ever done anything so simple, so romantic. Not that he'd taken her hand, but that the gesture had been natural as if his subconscious couldn't resist her.

They got into the elevator and rode first to the floor of her room. He walked her to her door and stopped. As if he just noticed he held her hand, he looked at their entwined fingers and then into her eyes.

The connection was so electric, it hurt to hold his gaze. His dark orbs kept secrets, made promises.

"You know I want to kiss you right now."

"Yes." Because she wanted him to kiss her, too. She wanted to pick up where they'd left off at the castle. Before they'd ruined it in the car by talking about reality—

Reality? That was three thousand miles away, across an ocean. Technically, they were alone in a hotel on another continent.

And as he'd said, no one needed to know about any of this.

If she looked at this the right way, that statement in the car was like an unspoken pact not to speak of anything that happened on this trip—

Including what happened right now.

The moment stretched out between them. A choice. Kiss him. Maybe even make love with him. And then—

And then...

Go home and pretend nothing had happened?

Have her face turn red every time they said hello at one of Seth's parties? Feel awkward if they met at a coffee shop or passed on the street?

Or create a bond? Maybe fall in love the way her mom had and pine for him when he dropped her off at her condo tomorrow and then disappeared into the noise of Manhattan. After all, he was the one who'd said their feelings were wrong. Acting on the sexual attraction aspects would only confuse a time in her life that should be about the joy of pregnancy and preparing to become a mom.

She had a responsibility to the little life inside her. That was where her focus should be.

Turning away wasn't easy, but nothing about this situation was easy. That was why she avoided feelings. Getting hurt? Disappointing others? Those were things she didn't do.

So maybe not all the lessons she'd learned from dealing with her dad were useless?

She waved her key card across the lock to activate it. Turning the knob, she said, "Good night."

The door opened, and she stepped inside her room without a backward glance, her heart splintering with pain. The price of keeping her focus and her dignity was a wave of loneliness the likes of which she'd never felt before.

In bed an hour later, after a long bath, she wondered if he was thinking about her and knew he was. She had no idea what hummed between them, but if it was anything like the emotions that her mother had felt, it wasn't reliable.

And that was what she had to keep telling herself. She'd seen love firsthand and knew it frequently hurt people.

She forced her eyes closed. Quieted her

mind. And eventually fell into a deep sleep. She had no dreams about Trent following her with a dog on a leash that kept getting tangled in the wheels of her twins' stroller. Her mind went totally blank, totally black.

Her phone woke her hours later. She answered with a groggy, "Hello."

"This is the front desk. The extra luggage ordered by Mr. Sigmund is being brought to your room now."

Instantly awake, she scooted up in bed. "Extra luggage?"

"He said something about a ball gown."

"Oh." A ball gown wouldn't fit into the carry-on she'd been stuffing with clothes for days. His remembering that, ordering the bigger case, could have caused her to swoon at his consideration, but they'd talked about this the night before. He'd said what they felt was wrong. And she'd cemented that belief when she'd walked away from a kiss, maybe even a one-night stand. She couldn't let her thoughts go backward.

"Thank you."

As soon as she'd disconnected the call, her

phone rang again. Expecting it to be the concierge, she said, "Yes?"

"It's me. Trent. I take it you got the call about
the extra suitcase?" Trent sounded like he'd
been up and about for hours.

"Yes. Thank you."

"You're welcome. I bought a case big enough
that you can store the gown and all the rest
of your clothes and ditch the smaller case if
you want, so you're just handling one bag,
not dragging two. That was the good news.
Here comes the bad. My new assistant only
arranged for the rental car through last night.
Apparently, an agent for the company picked it
up this morning. My longtime assistant, Ashley, got us another one, but it won't be here
until noon."

She sat up, coming to full alert. "Noon?"

"We should have left at seven."

"Seven?" She glanced at the clock. It was
after nine. No wonder he sounded awake.

"I thought you'd want to get an early start."

"Then why'd you let me sleep in?"

"I was waiting for you to call me."

The wistfulness in his voice reminded her
that he'd wanted to kiss her the night before,

but she'd decided that anything, even something temporary between them, wasn't right, and she'd left him in the hall outside her door.

"I slept in." She licked her suddenly dry lips. "Give me ten minutes and I'll meet you in the lobby. We can eat breakfast in the hotel restaurant."

"I've had breakfast."

Oh. She almost said it but recognized that refusing a kiss the night before had set things in motion on his end, too. She'd drawn the line in the sand and he wouldn't argue, wouldn't even intrude on her day. He'd simply do what he'd set out to do: help his friend's sister. They'd found Pierre, she'd said her peace and now Trent would take her home.

"Why don't you have breakfast in your room and then a leisurely walk while we wait for the replacement rental?"

He didn't want to have breakfast with her or even hang out while they waited for their new rental car. Because she'd walked away from a kiss.

Or maybe after she'd walked away, he'd thought it through, the way she had, and realized even a one-night stand wouldn't work?

She didn't think that she'd hurt him or insulted him. He was too strong and too smart to get offended.

Unless he thought she hadn't liked their kiss...

That couldn't be true. She hadn't let him end it. She'd kept him where he was. Took what she wanted. Absorbed every wonderful sensation.

She suddenly wanted to tell him that. She wanted to put all her cards on the table and set things right. She didn't want him angry with her. She didn't want him distanced from her—

But wouldn't that just dredge up everything she'd settled when she walked away?

She swallowed down the need to set things right in favor of the hope that there was a woman out there who could help heal his wounds, the kind of woman her brothers had found.

"Okay. I'll call room service. Just let me know when the rental car gets here."

"Will do."

She didn't hear one iota of regret in his voice—

Of course not. Would he want her to know

that she'd disappointed him? Big, strong, genius that he was, he wouldn't fail publicly. He would save his pride.

She disconnected the call and tossed the covers off the bed. She was done thinking about this.

The guy was sweet, kind, considerate, handsome…

He deserved a woman who could appreciate all that.

Trent disconnected the call and threw his cell phone to the sofa. He wasn't about to get angry with a new assistant who'd made a mistake, but he'd mapped all this out the night before. Get up at six, order breakfast from room service to eat while he read his usual newspapers, shower and dress and call Sabrina just before seven. That way she'd have time to get dressed while room service delivered her breakfast, but nothing else.

He'd planned topics for the drive to the airstrip.

Then he had a ton of things to read and evaluate on the plane.

Nothing about their time together would slip out of his control.

Because he'd finally figured out that *he* was the wild card. Sabrina was perfect Sabrina McCallan all the time. He was the one who kept losing hold of his emotions and doing things like kissing her or telling her he wanted to kiss her. He couldn't believe he'd done it. But when he'd made that backhanded comment about wondering how things could be different if just one thing had changed or if they'd met at a different time, her eyes had shifted, gone soft with yearning as if she'd applied the possibility to them and she wanted to know.

His mind started rolling through potential outcomes, and their odds weren't good for anything long-term, but for one totally inappropriate minute he'd believed they could have one night.

One night.

One blissful, perfect night that could live in their memories forever. As surely as he knew his first, middle and last names, he knew one night with her would stay with him for the rest of his life. And he wanted it.

He'd asked for the kiss, hadn't taken, knowing this had to be a mutual decision but she'd kept her cool and walked into her room.

After a restless night, he'd recognized she'd been correct. So he planned the rest of their time together down to the last minute.

Then his assistant had made a mistake—

He refused to let the late arrival of a rental throw him. He still had the conversation topics, still had the work that needed to be done. He would be a rock. He would not fall victim to the curiosity that constantly flitted through Sabrina's eyes. He would not see her as someone who'd never experienced real romance. He would hold his heart in check, refusing to let it soften over the longing that sometimes quivered through her voice. Most of all, he would resist the temptation to be the guy who showed her the difference between making love and being someone's lover.

That was what kept throwing him. She could say one thing with her mouth while her eyes told a totally different story. Which meant he had to be so strong, she wouldn't even notice how hard he had to work at ignoring the curiosity, the yearning, she telegraphed with her eyes.

His personal assistant, Ashley, called an hour later. "I got confirmation that you'll have an SUV at noon."

"Thanks. And don't be too hard on Makenzie for getting the rental car information wrong. People make mistakes."

Ashley laughed. "She didn't have her head in the game. She needs to learn to take things to their logical conclusion. If you needed a car to get from the airstrip to the hotel, you'll need it to get back to the airstrip. This wasn't one of those times she should have arranged to have your car picked up at the hotel."

"My schedule and my needs fluctuate so much when I travel that the person making the arrangements really has to pay attention. Think she's going to catch on?"

"She's smart. This mistake embarrassed her enough that she'll never do it again. Plus, we don't fire people. We give them a chance to grow into the job."

He chuckled. Ashley didn't miss a trick. Not even when he tested her. "Exactly. I'll see you next week."

"Going to the lake?"

"Maybe." Retreating to the lake wasn't a bad idea. He needed some time to himself, some time to get his priorities in line and his emotions in check. "The trip was a little jarring. I don't usually fly to three countries in four days. I may need to sit in one place an entire week to feel normal."

She laughed again. "Okay. See you *next* Monday."

He disconnected the call and shook his head. "A little jarring?" He should change his impression of Sabrina McCallan from class in Chanel to temptation in Chanel. But this wasn't about sex or his need. This was about her eyes. Her longing. Her curiosity. A curiosity she didn't want to satisfy. At least not with him.

He called her and told her their rental would arrive at noon and she said she'd be ready. Her formal, no-nonsense tone continued while they loaded their things into the SUV and for the first fifteen minutes of the drive.

That should have pleased him. As long as she was standoffish, he wouldn't make any slipups. But all he saw was a woman so curious about love and romance that she had to hide behind an overly polite facade.

Fine. Whatever.

He still refused to give in to temptation.

He internally screamed that at his hormones, which were absolutely positive he could lure her to him. Or at least show her a good time. Show her the way a woman should be treated. They'd both gotten sidetracked over everything that had happened the night before, and he'd forgotten that the last man she'd dated hadn't been kind to her. And he wouldn't fix that by ravaging her.

Sabrina's voice brought him out of his reverie. "Sky's getting dark."

They were far away from Dublin now, taking a country road that would lead to another country road and then another, which would ultimately get them to the super private airstrip where his jet sat.

"What's the weather supposed to be?"

"I don't know." She pulled out her phone. "I haven't looked at the weather in days. But I can check."

Using her thumbs, she hit apps and typed things and after a few seconds she cursed.

He stole a glance at her. "What?"

"I found something with radar and there's a band of thunderstorms coming our way."

He brushed it off. "Some rain."

"Lots of rain."

"We'll be fine."

CHAPTER NINE

SABRINA DIDN'T THINK SO.

"There are red bands in the streaks of yellow."

His brow puckered. "Red?"

"The guide says red means heavy rain. Like inches."

Three huge drops hit the windshield, then ten or twenty that turned into hundreds. Within minutes the rain was an onslaught so strong and so fast the sound of it drumming on the roof of the SUV was like thunder.

She scrambled to swipe down on the screen to read the rest of the information on the weather page. She gasped. "It's the tail end of a hurricane."

He gaped at her. "A hurricane?"

"More like a tropical storm now. They thought it was going to hit much farther north." She showed him her phone just as the wind whipped their rented SUV. The rain fell in thick sheets that prevented her from seeing the road. "This isn't good."

He drove the vehicle to the berm. "Let me have a look at that."

He took the phone, read the weather page and whistled. "Did you see the part about this being a slow-moving storm? This rain will last at least a day."

He tossed her phone back to her and pulled out his. He pressed two buttons then said, "We're in a huge storm here, Ashley. Something that was supposed to hit north of us but must have shifted. Look it up and tell us what we're dealing with."

"Give me a sec." A young woman's voice entered the interior of the SUV through the speaker. The *click, click, click* of computer keys followed it. "Ireland is getting the end of a hurricane." Another few clicks. "Wow. The predicted rainfall is not good. A couple of inches an hour. I hope you're still at the hotel."

The concern in Ashley's voice gave Sabrina a weird feeling. Not exactly jealousy. More like a recognition of how much Trent's assistant liked and respected him. The warmth flowing through her was pleasure that he'd found an employee who appreciated him. Then she realized an easygoing guy like Trent would surround himself with people with his same values. Picturing it, his personality and life came into sharp focus for her. He genuinely liked people. He really did want everyone to enjoy life.

"Actually, Ashley, we're in the middle of nowhere."

"Find shelter," Ashley said, the sound of the keys clicking punctuating her words. "Does Sabrina have an international phone?"

Surprised, Sabrina looked at him. He shrugged and said, "Yes."

"Use it to bring up General Maps. It will pick up your location on a satellite and find the nearest town."

Even as Trent said, "Great. Thanks," Sabrina brought up General Maps. Their location appeared on the screen, in the center of a map of the area.

"There's nothing for miles."

Trent said, "That's okay. I'll call you when we're settled, Ashley."

"Hey, I don't get to see how this turns out?"

"It's rain," Trent said, reassuring her. "We'll be fine."

The odd feeling hit Sabrina again. The connection between Trent and his assistant didn't sound romantic, but there was clearly affection there. And why not? Trent was a great guy. But hearing the concern in his assistant's voice was another proof of what she'd been learning about Trent in the past few days.

He wasn't just good-looking and rich. He was unique, wonderful.

Trent disconnected the call and turned to Sabrina. "We're going to have to continue moving until we find shelter."

"Okay." She nodded at her phone. "I can keep the maps program on-screen. If it comes up with something like a town or a farm or something, we'll know in time to look through the sheets of rain for it."

"That's the spirit." He blew his breath out on a sigh and pulled the gearshift into Drive. "Let's go."

Ten nerve-racking minutes later, shelter appeared in the form of a castle at the top of a small hill.

Sabrina shook her head. "A castle? You've got to be kidding."

He peeked at her. "Beggars can't be choosers."

As if to reinforce his statement, the wind knocked at the big SUV again. Rain pummeled the windshield.

She pressed her hand to her stuttering heart. The castle hadn't come up on the maps app. But nothing had, and the rain had created rivers and ponds along the road and in the grass beside it. He was right. They had no choice but to check this out.

He turned to go up the hill. "Here's the plan. When I stop, you jump out and run for the door."

She nodded.

Trent drove to the top of the hill and stopped the vehicle. She punched her shoulder against her door. It popped open and she leaped out into the driving rain.

The castle's big wooden double doors were protected by a small overhang, but not enough to shelter her completely. Wind butted against her. Rain drenched her back.

She frantically searched for a doorbell.

When she didn't find one, she grabbed the knocker and banged it against the wood.

No answer.

Trent raced up beside her, rolling their luggage behind him. She frowned, puzzled by his priorities.

"If we're going to be at the mercy of the owner of this castle, the least we can do is wear dry clothes."

Everything in their bags had been worn. That morning they'd put on the last of the outfits purchased for them by his personal shopper.

"All our clothes are dirty."

"Maybe the castle will have a washer?"

When no one answered after Sabrina's second knock, Trent set the suitcases on the stoop and banged the knocker against the door several times.

No one came.

He sucked in a breath. "Did you see a light when we drove up?"

Rain had soaked his shirt and dripped from his now-short hair. She couldn't help thinking of his assistant. What would it be like to work with this gorgeous man every day and not get a crush on him? She couldn't imagine it, until she realized Trent wouldn't flirt or make sexy talk with an employee. He'd create a safe environment for his workers.

Which meant every flirty word he'd said to her had been honest, genuine. He felt things for her that he didn't feel for other women. The thought filled her with equal parts of joy and confusion.

And an odd feeling of being special. But not in the way her mom and dad thought her special or the world thought her special. In a way that was more intimate. More real. She didn't have to jump through hoops for this man or be perfect. Lord knows she hadn't been anywhere near perfect. She'd been nervous about her pregnancy at the wedding, gotten angry about Pierre's ranch, told Pierre off, then walked out like queen of the world. A little too proud of herself.

And still he'd kissed her.

He'd said he couldn't help kissing her.

"If there's a light on, then we know someone's home but if there isn't, we're going to have to think outside the box."

She swallowed hard as the importance of

Trent's feelings overwhelmed her. No pretense. No funny stuff. He just liked her.

Her. Exactly as she was.

She shook her head. "No. No light."

He leaned out of the small shelter and surveyed the castle, then popped back in. "I'm going to assume no one is home."

"Really? Just because of no light being on?"

"No. Because we can't stand out here forever. Besides—" He took a credit card from his wallet. "I've heard a lot of these castles are abandoned."

Breaking into a house wasn't what her brothers would do. It certainly wasn't what her mom would want her to do. Yet, there was something so elemental about it that her heart skipped a beat. The man was just so damned male.

She looked at the driving rain then back at him. "So we're about to take refuge in a stone monstrosity that might be full of cobwebs?"

"You have a better idea?"

She considered telling him they should get back on the road, away from all the temptations that would dog them if they were alone in a house for God knew how long. But common sense and the pelting rain told her they'd never make it to the airstrip. Already the castle's grassy hill was shiny with water and puddles. The back roads they would take to the airstrip could get washed out, and if they did make it, they probably wouldn't be able to take off. They'd spend the next twenty-four hours in a cold, dark, dank hangar.

There was no good choice here.

"Get us inside."

He couldn't budge the lock of the thick wooden doors with his credit card, and he raced out into the storm, hoping to find another way in. After what seemed like hours of being bombarded by wind and rain, the front door opened.

Sabrina ducked inside, dragging her big suitcase. He grabbed his and yanked it in before he closed the door behind them.

Windows provided very little light but what furniture Sabrina could see was draped with dust covers.

"I don't see any cobwebs."

She glanced around cautiously. "Oh, I'm sure they're here."

He laughed. "You're going to have to look at

this like an adventure." He disappeared into the darkness.

She heard a few clicks.

"Either the place doesn't have electricity, or the storm has already taken out the power."

She shivered as he walked over to her. Stuck in a scary castle with a gorgeous, thoughtful, tempting man and no lights. No nothing, but each other.

He grabbed the handle of her suitcase. "Come on. Let's go upstairs and get out of these wet clothes."

The image that brought almost made her groan. She knew he wasn't propositioning her but that was how her silly brain took it.

Working to get her thoughts on track again, she said, "What if the owners were just out shopping and they come back?"

He sent her a patient look. "Seriously. People don't put dust covers on furniture when they go to the supermarket." He ran his finger along the newel post at the bottom of a curved stairway. "I'd say that's months' worth of dust, not days or even weeks. Months. This is probably somebody's country retreat."

She pulled in a shaky breath. It was dark,

and she was cold and wet. She didn't feel like meeting an irate owner, too. But what he'd said made sense. Thick dust and covers on the furniture added up to a uninhabited house.

No, not a house. *A castle.*

If she hadn't been so cold, she might have laughed.

She started up the stairs, using her phone to light the way. Trent added his and the entire stairway came into view. Relieved, she did laugh.

"What's so funny?"

"We're in a castle."

"So? We were in a castle last night."

"But that one was renovated. This one might actually be abandoned."

"Maybe because it's haunted."

They reached the top of the stairs and found huge webs of dust arching from one side to the other in the second-floor hall. She winced. "No self-respecting ghost would stay in this castle."

"He would if this was his home hundreds of years ago and he'd died in a bloody battle to save it."

She groaned. "Now you're just trying to scare me."

"Let's see what's behind door number one."

Because he dragged the suitcases behind him, she opened the door and turned her phone light into the bedroom. A double bed, dresser and chair were draped in dust covers.

"Not very big."

She smirked. "Big enough for one of us."

"I think it might be smarter if we limited our messing things up to a room or two. Like one bedroom and the kitchen."

That brought more of those weird thoughts again. Snuggling together with the sound of the wind and rain outside their window. Kissing. Peeling off wet clothes.

He glanced around. "Right now I'd like to put on a dry shirt, take my phone light and investigate the place."

Thank God he'd interrupted those thoughts. She sucked in a breath. "If we both go, you'll have more light."

"Or we'll simply run down both phone batteries. I think we need to start conserving power."

Her eyes widened. "What are you saying?"

"That there's a possibility we'll be here more than one day. And if there's no electricity, there's no charging phones."

She breathed a sigh of relief. "I thought you were hinting we might need our phones to call for help."

He winced. "That, too."

Real fear sent shivers through her. "Oh."

"I could be dead wrong. But it's always better to be safe rather than sorry."

Of course! He was thinking ahead not out of fear but out of caution.

She felt ridiculous for being a ninny and blamed it on the darkness combined with the sound of the storm buffeting the castle. And the attraction that kept intruding itself into her thoughts.

"You're right."

He tossed their luggage to the bed. "I'm going to look for things like a generator or even a fireplace that works. But first I need to get out of this shirt."

She headed for the door, her phone lighting the way. "Okay."

"Where are you going?"

"Out. So you can change."

"Not if it means you have to use your phone. Take the dust cover off the chair or have a seat on the bed, then turn it off."

She sighed. "I'm just going out to the hall while you change."

"Why? You said yourself the house is totally dark. Besides, you've seen me without a shirt."

She had. That was what had started her confusion. Until that minute, he'd been Ziggy, her brother's wealthy but goofy friend. Now he was a sexy, adult male *Trent.*

She yanked off the dust cover, sat on the chair, then hit the button to turn off her phone and hoped it really was dark enough inside the castle that she wouldn't see him.

It was…but she heard him sniff loudly. "This is the shirt I changed into on the plane when we arrived in Paris. It still smells okay."

"At this point, I think body odor is the least of our worries."

"True." A few seconds passed as he probably wrestled into the shirt, then turned his phone toward her. "All right. I'm going to investigate the house. Do you want to come along or are you okay sitting here in the dark?"

"My clothes are wet too. I'll change while you're gone."

"Good thinking. Wish me luck. I'm hoping to find a generator."

After he left, she inched her way to the bed and found her suitcase. But Trent's sat open beside it on the dusty bed. She ran her hand along the folded clothes, marveling that he was so tidy, then at the feel in the fabrics. Denim, cotton and the silk of the shirt he'd worn with his tuxedo. As soon as she touched it, she felt every blissful second of the kiss they'd shared the night before, after she'd talked to Pierre.

She snatched her hand away. That was just stupid. Stupid. Stupid. She had never gone through a girlie phase and couldn't believe she was starting now.

Running her hand along clothes he'd worn, feeling things she could usually shut down, liking things about him she'd never looked for in a man before?

Was she nuts?

Hadn't she talked herself out of all this the night before?

She opened her suitcase and found the shirt she'd worn in Paris, along with a scarf to use as a shawl. The castle was old, and the darkness made it feel colder. She rummaged for something to dry her damp hair and pulled out one of the two pair of pajamas Trent's personal shopper had sent over for her when they were in Barcelona.

Thinking of Barcelona reminded her of dancing. Feeling young and free in the silly blue sparkly dress that she'd ended up liking. She remembered the couple dancing beside them, their sensuous kiss, remembered her guess that Trent would be a demanding kisser and got goose bumps.

No. She wasn't nuts. *He* was different. So different than Pierre. So different than most of the men she met that she was having trouble acclimating.

Satisfied with that explanation, she ran the pajama top along the bottom of her long hair, the part that had somehow gotten more rain, telling herself that her sound reasoning had her back to normal.

Ten minutes later he returned to the bedroom and flicked on the light.

Sabrina said, "You found a generator!"

"Nope. Breakers were off, which goes to

prove that whoever lives here, doesn't live here full-time. Come on, let's go explore the kitchen. I don't expect to find much, but there might be some canned beans or soup."

They left the room and headed down the stairs. Though thick with dust, the corridor leading to the steps had wooden walls, painted white. Wood trim accented the high ceilings. Walnut steps, railing and newel post were brightened by white spindles in the stairway that matched the wood walls.

"Now that we can use our chargers, I can turn my phone back on."

He snorted. "Seriously? Are you one of those people who can't live without her phone?"

She walked down the final three steps, following him when he turned right to go through the huge foyer. With the space now lit, she could see the flagstone flooring, the high ceilings and long, thin walnut table that ran almost the entire length of the wall beneath the stairway. Looking at the ornate chandelier, with light poking through its dusty crystals, she imagined that in its prime, this entryway was amazing.

She sighed. "I like to Google things."

For that he paused and faced her. "Really?"

"Sure." She displayed her phone. "With this in my hand, I know everything or at least have access to it."

"You're pretty smart without that phone."

Pleasure washed through her at his compliment. "I know some things."

He turned and began walking again. "You know a lot of things."

"I should. Not only did I grow up with a dad who quizzed my brothers at the dinner table, but I mentor some very smart entrepreneurs."

They passed through a dusty sitting room. A cover draped a long, traditional sofa. The stone fireplace across from two wing chairs desperately needed repairs. The same was true for the fireplace in the equally dusty dining room, a long space with a table that seated thirty. She counted the high backs of chairs beneath another dust cover. Rough wood floors had been prettied up with area rugs that looked to be from the nineteen hundreds. Walls had been framed out and dry-walled or plastered, creating deep borders around the windows. Dusty pillows sat in the corners, making the wide sills look like reading nooks.

"I'll bet this place is fabulous when it's clean. It doesn't even look to need much remodeling."

"Remodeling?"

"I love to decorate."

"From the look of your condo, I'd say you're pretty good at it. So if that's what you like to do, how'd you decide to start a nonprofit that helps startups?"

She laughed. "I was thumbing my nose at my dad. He didn't see me as a businesswoman? Well, then I'd have a hand in running hundreds of businesses."

Stepping into an old-fashioned kitchen with wooden cabinets and a long wooden table, no island, no granite, just old-fashioned white appliances, Trent said, "That's brilliant."

"Once he saw what I could do, he asked me to join the family business, but I could envision him making me a vice president then never giving me any work. I'd be a showpiece…maybe a token woman." She shook her head. "I wouldn't have it. Besides, I don't bail on my friends."

He studied her face for a few seconds. "No. I don't think you do."

She sucked in a breath, said what had been on her mind awhile, "Obviously, you don't, either."

"So we have something in common?"

"I think we have a lot in common."

Silence stretched between them. Gazes locked, they studied each other as if waiting for the other to say something.

But she didn't know what to say. They were forming a bond, or maybe a friendship. It was so much sweeter, richer, than anything she'd ever felt for a man that longing billowed from her chest to her toes. She'd give anything to be able to test this, to try it. To see what it felt like to be with someone not out of convenience or for fun…but for real.

For real?

Real was what her mother had…a husband with a temper and three confused kids.

She did not want real… Did she?

CHAPTER TEN

SABRINA ALMOST GROANED when she realized she couldn't answer that question with a resounding, "No."

Seeming oblivious to her confusion, Trent walked to the cabinets, opened two and found only dishes. "We might have to eat the plates."

Glad they weren't staring in each other's eyes anymore, Sabrina opened a cabinet door. "Or we could go a day without food."

He turned on the tap. "There's water."

"Oh, I can shower!" She walked to a full-size door, opened it and displayed a pantry. "I see beans."

He laughed. "Good."

She walked into the closet-size room lined with shelves. "Chicken soup! I love chicken soup."

"Me, too. Now that we know there's food,

let's finish our tour. I'd like to see the rest of this place."

"Seriously? You're willing to risk the dust?"

"Who cares about dust? Besides, you said you were going to shower."

It wasn't like they had a lot of other things to do, and occupying themselves with exploring the castle was a lot better than talking.

"Okay, let's go."

Because they'd entered the kitchen through the left, they took the door on the right and found themselves in a butler's pantry. Two rows of cabinets were made from the same white wood that created the stairway walls. The same walnut stain that adorned the stair rail trimmed the cabinet doors.

"This is huge."

He looked around. "Everything needs to be painted."

She ran her finger through the dust of a countertop. "Or maybe just cleaned."

He opened the door at the end of the room.

Expecting to see another sitting room, she gasped when she saw the enormous dining hall. With ceilings as tall as the ones in the entryway, the same flagstone floors and a table long enough to seat a hundred, the room was the first of the space to really feel like it belonged in a castle.

Her voice echoed around her as she spoke. "This is fabulous." The stone fireplace was twice the size of those in the living room and sitting room. The high ceiling boasted wood beams stained the same walnut color as the stairway rail in the entryway and the trim of the cabinets in the butler's pantry. At least a forty-foot space sat empty beside the long table.

"I'm guessing that space is for dancing," Trent said. "I'll bet they host parties here."

"Balls," Sabrina said whimsically. "With women in flowing dresses and men in those ruffled shirts."

He laughed. "You might think you're pragmatic, but I still say you're a romantic."

She wished. Because if she were a romantic, she'd have kissed him the night before. She'd be laughing and flirting, not looking for dust so she'd have something to comment on. She'd be giving in to the longings that swept through her, acting on things she'd never believed in, when they shared a bed that night.

Her thoughts froze. What if she wasn't strong enough tonight to resist that pull? Would she toss away decades of common sense for a few hours of wonderful?

She cleared her throat. "You know... Now that we have lights, maybe we could commandeer a second bedroom."

He looked over at her and her heart jumped to her throat. No man had ever given her that look before. His full lips had thinned. His sharp eyes held her in place.

Okay. He clearly did not like her suggestion.

"I'm just saying that with light and electricity we can clean up after ourselves. Maybe even wash the sheets before we leave."

His head tilted as his eyes searched hers. "Sure. That makes sense."

Disappointment in herself rumbled through her and she almost cursed. She was such a coward. She should have said, "Hey, I really like you. But we're not right for each other and I think sleeping in the same bed would be just a bit too tempting."

That was what strong Sabrina McCallan

would do. *Honesty* was her watchword. Not dodging things. But though Trent was probably the easiest man in the world to talk to, what she had to say wasn't simple or easy. Any time a man had tempted her before this, it was purely physical. She couldn't deny there was something more with Trent and if she explained it he would realize just how enticing he was to her.

And that would make her vulnerable...the way her mom had been.

Except Trent wasn't like her father. He wasn't harsh or demanding or even critical.

He was accepting, spontaneous, kind...

Double doors led outside, but rather than open them to the rain, Trent went to the kitchen, found some cloths and washed a space for them to peer through.

Benches sat along a stone walk in what had probably once been a beautiful garden.

"I'll bet this was magnificent in its prime."

She peeked at him. "Makes me itch to get my hands on it and fix it up."

"And host a ball?"

She blew her breath out. "I wouldn't even have time to make a guest list, let alone remodel this place enough to invite friends, let alone host a ball."

She stopped, disgusted with herself. Trent wasn't anything like her dad, and avoiding the truth with him was shameful.

She squeezed her eyes shut, then popped them open and caught his gaze. "I don't want to think about remodeling this place because it will never happen. Spinning fantasies is a waste of time. Since I'm rolling with the truth here, I might as well also admit I don't want to sleep in the same bed with you because I like you."

His expression shifted but he said nothing.

"I think it's just a little too much like tempting fate for us to be that close."

One of his eyebrows rose. "Afraid you'll ravage me?"

"Don't belittle what I feel."

"Okay." His voice grew soft, serious. "I won't. Let's go upstairs and look for another room."

Her breathing stopped. She couldn't tell if it was from disappointment that he hadn't argued or relief that he hadn't argued. Anytime her mom disagreed with her dad he'd exploded—

But she'd already decided Trent wasn't like her father. Maybe his reaction to finding a second room was the true test of that?

They found a back stairway and ambled up. At the top were two large guest rooms, each with a private bath.

"Whoever owns this place, he was smart when he remodeled."

"Everything is rather convenient."

He strolled around the room and she watched for signs that he was angry and not letting it show.

"They probably cut out a bedroom or two to make the extra baths."

His genuine interest in the castle took away her concern about his anger. If he'd been angry, he'd pushed it aside. But she didn't think he'd been angry. He might not have liked her suggestion that they sleep in separate rooms, but he'd accepted it.

It wasn't as if she hadn't dealt with an even-tempered man before. She met lots of them at her nonprofit. She'd simply never been in a relationship with one.

Of course, Pierre had been her longstanding adult boyfriend. There'd been no reason to think of dating in years.

The final guest room was like the first two, but the third-floor master suite was enormous.

Trent peered around. "I'm guessing this is at least half the floor. I'm also guessing we're going to find a super-huge bathroom and walk-in closet."

"I'm thinking dressing room."

The master closet was a combination closet and dressing room. Everything was old, worn. But that didn't take away from the beauty of the space. She could almost see a husband and wife dressing, laughing and chatting with each other.

She shook her head to clear it of the image. "This is lovely." But the mood of the vision stayed with her. This was a house made with love. She could feel the happiness that even the dust and time couldn't bury.

Damn it. She loved this house. And she didn't understand her unexpected connection to something so far out of the realm of possibility. She wasn't a woman who spun fantasies, wished for fanciful things.

She was honest, sincere, hardworking… normal.

Or maybe not so normal if she couldn't even fathom being in a relationship with someone she didn't have to manage.

She turned to Trent, who was examining the craftsmanship of the dressing room built-ins.

"I think I'll take one of the smaller bedrooms. You can have the one our luggage is in."

He shrugged. "Doesn't matter to me. I can just as easily bring my suitcase to another room like yours."

There was that easygoing nature again. A guy who didn't have to compromise because he wasn't overly sensitive or demanding.

"Okay. Either way."

"I'll move my stuff later, after we eat." He paused. "Unless you're hungry now?"

"No. I'm fine." A thought hit her, and she politely said, "Unless you're hungry now?"

"Nope. I'm good for a few hours."

Silence spun out between them until she realized he was waiting for her to make a move. She strode out into the empty corridor. This is what she got for being honest: a stiff, formal atmosphere that seemed to suck the life out of everything. She shouldn't have told him why she didn't want to sleep with him. She should have let him draw his own conclusions…

But that didn't sit right, either. He'd been open, honest with her all along and she'd been open with him. It was only when sleeping in the same bed came into the picture that her reactions got muddled.

Not wanting this weird politeness to be the rest of their afternoon, she said, "Want to explore some more?"

He sniffed a laugh. "Dust phobia leaving?"

"It must be, because I'm suddenly curious to see if there's a dungeon or a tower where an old lord held women captive."

He hooted with laughter. "You have one hell of an imagination."

She almost told him about the Irish aristocracy she envisioned getting ready for a ball in the dressing room, but he'd only call her a romantic again. Just thinking about it made her heart hurt. Had she missed out because she wasn't a romantic? Did she not know how to deal with a normal man because she hadn't spun fantasies?

She couldn't even speculate. She simply knew she wanted her mind on something that didn't confuse her so much.

She pointed down a hall that veered off to the left. "I'll bet that leads to the back of the house and a stairway to a tower."

He snorted and motioned for her to go down the corridor.

They found four more bedrooms and a stairway that only led to a tower. She twirled around in a circle. Rain beat against a glass door, but she could see it led to a balcony.

"Well, what do you know? You don't just get your tower…you also get a balcony." He rubbed his elbow against the glass to clear it. "I'll bet you can see for miles up here."

"I'll bet this would make a great master bedroom."

He glanced around. "Why give up the perfect master suite that's already downstairs?"

"Then maybe I'd make this a reading room."

"Why not just let it be a tower?"

"Because it should be something special."

"A tower is pretty special."

She winced. "Sorry. I'm probably seeing this place in terms of remodeling because I have to do some remodeling in my condo and that's where my brain is focused. Everywhere I look I see a project."

He peered across the space at her. "Your ideas aren't bad."

"My ideas are spot-on." She turned in a circle again, taking in the space. "It's weird. I'm seeing the rooms, then seeing how I think they should be."

"Your brain is even busier than mine."

She shrugged. "Maybe. I never thought of it that way."

"Do you ever take a break?"

"That's what my paintings are about."

"Ah."

"What's that supposed to mean?"

"It means that you paint to relax, but then you monetize it."

She frowned. "I guess I do."

"Where do you vacation?"

She winced. "France."

"Oh, to see Pierre."

"You are really making me feel like a dull workaholic."

"Maybe you are a dull workaholic."

She gaped at him. "Seriously?"

His eyes fixed on the rain beyond the balcony, he said, "I'm not making fun or trying to tell you what to do with your life, but I'm noticing a serious lack of fun in everything you tell me."

"And I suppose your life's a real barrel of chuckles."

He faced her. "I fish. I travel. You met only four of my Barcelona friends. I have a whole network of friends in Spain. I also take my staff on corporate retreats to places like Fiji."

"I do fun things."

He snickered. "Okay. Name some."

"Well, doing art showings is fun."

"We already established that that's an extension of your work."

She tossed her hands. "Stop! I'm starting to feel boring."

"You're not boring. Your job alone sounds incredibly interesting. You just don't know how to stop working." He took a few steps toward her. "I understand that you don't want to tempt fate while we're here."

She held back a grimace, realizing he'd barely reacted when she'd told him she didn't want to sleep with him because he'd been thinking it through.

"But there's a part of me that wonders why fate threw us together like this. Since we can't have a relationship, the only possible reason for it is that fate wants me to show you how to have fun."

She considered that and couldn't quite figure out what he was suggesting. "Here? In a tropical storm?"

"The end of a tropical storm. We're not stranded forever. The rain's got to stop sometime. We could be out of here tomorrow morning." He met her gaze. "Not enough time to do something we'd regret, but enough time to enjoy each other's company."

When he put it like that it sounded innocent...and maybe even a little bit wonderful. "How would we have this fun?"

"Well, we could dress for dinner."

"Dress for dinner?" She thought of the Irish people in the bedroom again. When she pictured them, they were always laughing. Happy with each other. Her heart pinched. She couldn't even imagine those kinds of feelings...

The squeeze of her heart intensified into longing. But longing was so untrustworthy. Not a feeling she'd indulged the few times it had appeared. "Put on our good clothes just because we can?"

"Shower, put on our good clothes, fix our hair and use up an hour or two of all the time we have on our hands. Then pretend to be lord and lady of the manor having dinner in the great hall."

Now he was going overboard. "Eat our warmed-up beans in the great hall? Seriously?" The vision in her head morphed again. She saw them sitting at the long table, eating beans, laughing...

Nothing sexy, nothing foolish. Just two people getting to know each other. Maybe appreciating each other?

Temptation sent tingles up her spine. Before she and Trent had headed to Paris to find Pierre, she'd scoffed at the concept of real relationships. She would have made fun of his idea of dressing up and being silly with each other. Now she didn't merely believe real relationships existed; she wanted a taste. Just a taste. One night of being herself, enjoying herself with a man she genuinely liked. A man she found so attractive she sometimes caught her breath just looking at him.

"All right. Fine." She headed out of the tower. "If I'm going to waste time, I might as well see if I can't do something Marie Antoinette-ish with my hair."

"Not Marie Antoinette. She's French. Think Irish lass."

She laughed and walked down the three flights of stairs and Trent followed her. He fully intended not to tempt fate. No sleeping together. But now that he'd taken romance out of the equation, when that longing he kept seeing flitted through her eyes, he just wanted to make her happy.

Stupid. Since in her own little McCallan way she was happy. Content. Wealthy, with a fulfilling career.

And he was Trent Sigmund. Newly rich. Sometimes crass. Friend of her brother.

When she made the turn to go to her bedroom, he kept going down the stairs, on his way to the kitchen. At the very least, he was not letting her eat beans out of a can.

He walked into the pantry and found a treasure trove of interesting food. Spam, something his mother liked to cook, and which could be good if prepared correctly. The ever-popular beans. The soup Sabrina had found. Canned corn. Canned beans. Canned peas. Some boxes of pasta that weren't past their use-by date.

He could make a really good goulash out of this.

He grinned and walked to the butler's pantry, looking for a stash of alcohol. There was none. But after searching through rooms, opening doors that might hide a bar, he finally found one. It contained nothing fancy like tequila for margaritas, but there was wine.

Wine and goulash.

It wasn't posh or classy, but it would be delicious.

He pulled two bottles of the wine from behind the bar and took them to the refrigerator, which he plugged in.

Because he only had to shave, shower and slip into his tux, he did some cleaning in the great room while the wine chilled and Sabrina took her time doing whatever it was that caused women to need two or three hours to dress.

The wind and rain that had been pounding the house slowed, indicating the storm was moving on. They probably would be leaving the next morning. He walked up the stairs to take a shower and put on his tux, thinking his plan was a good one. They'd have fun eating and dancing in the great room, then go to separate rooms, sleep for a few hours and leave in the morning.

Actually, her suggestion that they sleep in different rooms had made the plan perfect. He could satisfy the need to erase the longing from her pretty blue eyes without worry that he'd hurt her.

What could possibly go wrong?

CHAPTER ELEVEN

TRENT TOOK OFF his tux jacket to make the goulash and set the table in the great room. But when everything was ready, he slipped it on again and stood at the bottom of the stairway, just about to go up and check on Sabrina, when she suddenly appeared at the top. Wearing the pretty blue gown she'd worn to Pierre's showing, with her long hair wild and free, she walked down the steps.

"I thought about what you said about the Irish lass." She pointed at her head. "So, I washed my hair and let it dry naturally."

"It's perfect." *She* was perfect. "You look like you could be running in a glen."

She laughed. "So that's how this is going to be? We're getting in character and staying there?"

"Sure." He stuffed his hands in his trouser pockets, so he couldn't indulge the need to touch her. "If you're going to be stranded, it's best to be stranded somewhere entertaining." He smiled when she reached the bottom of the steps. "I found wine."

She grinned. "I'm pregnant. Can't drink wine, remember?"

He winced. "Sorry. I'll look for juice or we can drink water. I also found pasta and canned veggies and made goulash with macaroni, beans and corn."

"Sounds interesting."

He motioned for her to go to the great hall. "Oh, I forgot there's Spam, too."

She stopped walking, turned and frowned at him. "What the hell is Spam?"

"Canned meat that's pretty tasty if you ignore the fact that it's probably a zillion calories and loaded with cholesterol."

"I'm starving so I'd be willing to overlook that."

Temptation overwhelmed common sense and he took her hand and tucked it in the crook of his elbow to escort her to their dinner. "I was hoping you would. Sometimes Spam can be delicious."

"I'm going to take your word on that."

They entered the great room and she gasped. "Oh, my gosh! This is fabulous."

He'd dusted the table and chairs, swept the floor, set out good china and found glasses and candles, giving her the luxury she was accustomed to…even if the dinner was a sort of poor man's feast.

He pulled out the chair catty-cornered from his, and she sat, arranging her dress around her.

"Give me one minute. I'm pretty sure I saw a bottle of sparkling apple juice in the bar."

He raced off and sure enough there were two bottles. He grabbed one and headed back to the great room.

As he took the seat at the head of the table, an odd sense of rightness enveloped him. A peace he'd never felt.

He blamed that on the discomfort he'd always experienced as a child. Any time the family did anything fancy, he was the fifth wheel. Sabrina made him feel part of things.

Not wanting to examine that too deeply, he opened the apple juice and poured two glasses. "Sorry it's warm."

"I'm sure it's fine." She took hers and sipped delicately then closed her eyes. "It's excellent."

"The owner of this house has weird tastes. The wine I'd found was excellent, but he also had canned veggies and Spam."

"Maybe he has kids." She glanced around. "I can picture this house filled with kids."

So could he. "It would be the perfect week-end house if it had a pool."

"There might be a pool behind the gardens, something we couldn't see because of the overgrowth." She smiled. "My family has a house in Montauk. Our pool is pretty far back. Actually, it's a hike to the pool. If it rained hard enough, you wouldn't be able to see it from the kitchen." She laughed. "The ocean's such a long walk from the house that Avery wouldn't stay there."

He frowned. "Really? She doesn't like a good walk?"

"She wasn't married to Jake at the time she was supposed to stay there. In fact, they were sort of fighting. McCallan Inc. was the biggest client of the law firm where Avery worked, and Jake was about to sue her to let him have a part in their baby's life. So the firm had to let her go because of conflict of interest."

He shook his head. "Your family does have its scandals."

"Without her job, she had to sell her condo and Jake suggested she live at our house in Montauk. But it was too big for her, too much house, too much furniture, too much everything and—" she changed her voice to mimic Avery "—too far from the ocean. So Jake made arrangements with Seth to let her stay in Seth's little cottage that was right on the beach." She smiled dreamily. "I think that's why she fell in love with him. He never forced our lifestyle on her. He found ways to make her happy."

Trent stared at her, seeing the romantic in her that she thought she kept hidden. He almost mentioned it again, but before he could, he saw her point about Jake and Avery. Jake didn't try to change the woman he loved because he loved her—exactly as she was.

In the same way Avery had stolen Jake's heart just as she was, Sabrina was stealing his. He wanted to please her, not change her.

They might not have forever but he wanted to leave her with good memories.

This dinner was his one shot.

"You really look pretty tonight."

The compliment went straight to Sabrina's heart. Her face flushed, but before she had to fumble with a reply, Trent reached for her plate and poured a ladleful of goulash onto it.

It looked a little crazy, a little sloppy, not quite soup, but not quite solid, either, but it smelled delicious.

He filled his own plate then motioned for her to take a bite.

Trying not to be too obvious about her slight fear of Spam, she cautiously filled her spoon with pasta, vegetables and Spam and slid it into her mouth.

Flavor exploded on her tongue. The odd mix of vegetables and pasta and Spam bathed her taste buds. "Wow."

"Wow good or wow bad?"

"Good! It's delicious. It reminds me a bit of jambalaya."

"You've been to the South."

"My mother was a belle."

He thought about that, thought about dignified but generous Maureen, who hosted balls, gave away millions of dollars and loved Seth so fiercely Trent had been envious. "I can see it."

"It's why she fit so well into New York high society. Might have been slightly different rules, but it was the same game."

"My mother was a schoolteacher."

Her gaze jumped to his. "No kidding!"

"My dad—stepdad—was a dock worker. They could stretch a nickel better than anyone I've ever met." He smiled at the memories. "I learned to manage money from them."

Sabrina studied him. He'd learned how to manage money from his parents, obviously loved them from the look of affection that came to his face. Yet, he'd never clicked with his stepdad.

"It's why I know how to cook things like goulash."

A million questions assaulted her. She sorted through them before she carefully said, "Your family sounds nice." Not a question, more like an opening for him to talk.

"They are very nice. But they are solidly

blue collar. Even the notion of expanding beyond their borough is uncomfortable for them. They like their block parties. They're active in their community. But that's kind of the point. They know who they are, like who they are."

"And you wanted more?"

"I wanted an education." He shrugged. "I didn't necessarily want to leave that life. I could live anywhere. I don't have a maid, just a cleaning service that comes in. I could keep my fancy cars in storage. No one has to know how much money I have." He laughed. "I could be the billionaire next door. But the truth is my family didn't want me around."

"That part sounds awful."

"It isn't when you realize that I hadn't fit for a while. I wasn't surprised when my stepdad turned down the house I'd bought for him and my mom." He paused, took a breath, then caught her gaze. "It made it official that I was out of sync with them."

"You make it sound so sterile. But I know it had to hurt."

"It did. Sometimes it still does. But everybody's supposed to grow up, to move on. I'm just the guy whose parents don't want him to come home for holidays."

Silence reigned as they ate a bite or two of goulash, took a sip or two of sparkling apple juice, then he laughed. "I'm making it sound horrible and it isn't. When I woke up the day after my stepdad turned down the house, I realized I could be whoever I wanted, do whatever I wanted."

She set down her spoon. "Make your own rules?"

"Why not? The old ones didn't work for me."

She sniffed. "The old ones don't really work for me, either."

"Then maybe you'd like to join me in the land where I decide what's good and bad, what's fun and what's not, and where I choose what I want to do and with whom."

"Not till after I hear some of the rules."

"Well, for one, you always have to be yourself…your real self."

She snorted. "I've been my mother's perfect daughter for so long I'm not really sure I know my real self."

"Maybe *this* is your real self."

She shook her head. "No. When I bought this gown, I tried on a red one I liked more."

"Really? Prettier than that?" He chuckled before he took a drink. "Because you look amazing in that one."

She took a sip of apple juice, letting his compliment sink into her soul. "The other was more beautiful. Red, with no back."

His brow wrinkled. "No back?"

"It was fantastic. It fit me the way the blue sparkly one your shopper picked out fit. But it had long sleeves and a dramatic dip in the back that stopped at the very top of my butt. It was artistic and passionate and when I put it on..." She glanced down at her plate, then back up at him. "I felt it. That indefinable thing that clicks in your soul."

Confusion filled his dark eyes. "So why didn't you get it?"

"Because I have blond hair and blue eyes and wearing the color blue makes me into this physically perfect picture."

He only stared at her.

"Blondes wear blue. We look good in blue."

"It sounds like you have a snapshot in your head that you keep recreating."

Her eyes widened. "That's it exactly."

He leaned back in his chair. "When it comes to people, I know my stuff. I might have missed that my stepfather would eventually nudge me out of my own family, but I hadn't missed that he'd always been standoffish with me. And being attuned to that made me attuned to people in a different way, and that translated to picking up on things that make me a good investor. I can see when a CEO's bumpy marriage is going to cause him to lose focus for his company or when a board of directors is getting cocky, taking risks that might devalue their corporation."

"Makes sense." She swirled the liquid in her glass. "When I interview potential clients, I look for rough patches in their personal lives. That doesn't necessarily count them out. If the client is strong and motivated, I can teach them how to work around personal troubles, so they don't affect their business."

"Another thing we have in common." He poured more apple juice into both of their glasses. "You should have bought the red dress."

She shook her head. "I was very close to

it. But I wanted to blend in at Pierre's show-ing, not stand out. Trust me, in that red dress I would have stood out."

They finished their goulash, polished off the first bottle of sparkling juice and opened a second.

"We should probably wash these dishes."

Trent pushed back his chair. "We'll get them in the morning. Right now I thought we'd dance."

"Dance?"

He pointed to the great room's dance floor. "I want the full experience. We can pretend we're at a ball."

He walked to her chair and pulled it out for her.

"Or we could pretend we're the lord and lady of the house."

"At a ball?"

"Or alone." She pictured it. Her laughing Irish couple from the dressing room. The hus-band and wife who would own a castle like this. "With the kids tucked in bed and the ser-vants in their quarters, they would dance."

And probably go upstairs and make love.

For the first time since Barcelona the idea

didn't scare her. It felt like the perfect ending to a trip that had absolutely changed her.

He studied her as he slid his phone from his jacket pocket. "Why am I getting the feeling that you've thought this through?"

She shrugged. "Maybe I have."

He found his playlist, the one filled with slow, romantic songs, then held out his hand to her. He didn't remind her that she was supposed to be pragmatic, not a dreamer. He liked this side of her, sensed that he was with the real Sabrina, the one who would have bought and worn the happy, artistic, sexy red dress.

Music filled the room. He led her to the dance floor and pulled her close. She melted into him and the sense of rightness he'd had at the beginning of the night drifted through him like the simple, easy notes of the song floating around them, creating a little world all their own.

He let himself soak up the feeling. He had lots of friends and girlfriends and employees who were friends. But he'd never had this closeness, this intimacy, with another person. He'd never wanted it. Never missed it.

But holding her now, he knew that when they went back to their separate worlds this dance would haunt him. Make him wish he'd found the courage to let this relationship evolve to its natural conclusion.

"Do you ever think that some people aren't meant for forever?"

He leaned back, looked into her eyes. "What do you mean?"

"My parents soured me on marriage. Pretty soon I'm going to have a child to raise. That's going to limit everything I do." She shrugged. "I don't know what I'm saying."

He thought he did. At least a little. She might be a romantic, but she didn't think she'd get the happily-ever-after.

But why mention it now?

Unless…

"Are you saying you think we aren't made for forever?"

She held his gaze. "You wondered why fate had thrown us together. Well, there's a part of me that knows. I've loved everything about tonight, but more than that, I really like you."

"I like you, too." Her simple declaration sent need rippling through him, and this time he didn't fight it. He dipped his head, kissed her slowly and thoroughly. "And?"

Her breath stuttered. "And aren't you just the tiniest bit curious about how this night should end?"

"I actually had a plan."

"You did?"

He spun them around once, then kissed her again. He hadn't taken his plan this far, but now that they were here, on the threshold of something amazing, the plan morphed, taking a wonderful turn. "I've decided to seduce you."

"Oh."

He kissed the lips forming the perfect, "Oh." Drew the kiss out languidly.

Slowed their dance steps to almost none so he could enjoy her taste, the softening of her body against his, the yearning of his own body for hers.

When he pulled away she looked sleepy-eyed and happy. "Maybe we should share that room after all."

"Maybe we should."

CHAPTER TWELVE

CAUGHT IN THE spell of his dark eyes, Sabrina stood frozen. He broke their dance hold, took her hand and led her to the table where he blew out the candles, then to the door, the stairway and the bedroom. Arousal joined her awareness of how male he was, how lucky she was to have this just one night.

But everything was so perfect, the strangest feelings flitted through her. Thoughts of forever inched into her conscious, forming the realization that this wasn't just a man she wanted, this was a man she could trust.

She shoved those thoughts aside. She didn't want them intruding on her perfect night when she knew one night might be all they got together.

She stood on her tiptoes and kissed him until there was no reality around her but darkness and Trent.

When they woke together the next morning, he pulled her close and kissed her before he jumped out of bed to go to the room where he'd stored his suitcase to get his toothbrush.

With morning light streaming in through the open curtains on the big windows, Sabrina knew she must have looked a fright, and while he was gone she ran into the private bath of her room to use her toothbrush and comb out the tangles of her hair.

But she stopped herself. She didn't hate her wild hair. She liked it. And, mysteriously, she looked like a woman Trent would date. Except she had a little more meat on her bones.

She combed her hair enough that it wasn't a mass of tangles and when he returned to the bedroom, wearing sweatpants but no shirt, she realized that with his now-short hair, he looked like the kind of guy she would date.

They'd always been these people. Just hidden under tons of misconceptions and a boatload of fears.

But why pick now to change…unless something about being together brought out the best in them?

He threw back the covers and patted the bed, indicating she should join him. She did. Willingly. Feeling a billion different things, the most confusing of which was the surety that this…being with him, wild hair, tight dresses, honest conversations…was her future. Her *destiny.*

If it hadn't felt so right, she might have argued with it.

And maybe she still should be careful, not let the happiness of making love to someone she truly loved cloud the truth. Especially since she'd told him the night before that she believed this was a one-time thing.

Still naked, she slid into bed and over to him. Something had happened the night before. Something wonderful.

And she wanted it.

Maybe she'd even fight for it—something so un-Sabrina-like she should have questioned it. But every time she tried, she would remember the night before and know with certainty she couldn't go back to being the person she'd been, but more than that she refused to go on without him.

* * *

He cuddled her against him and pulled the covers over them. He wasn't sure what had happened the night before but he wanted it.

He hadn't slept with a million women, but he'd slept with enough to know when something was special, perfect. He hoped Sabrina felt that, too, but if she hadn't, he had to figure out how to get her to see it.

Of course, he also realized he didn't have to do that today. Now that they'd found each other, they could date. He couldn't believe he'd thought that they couldn't. And he almost couldn't remember why he'd thought that.

The music of a mariachi band burst into the room. Leaning across him, Sabrina grabbed her phone from the bedside table and winced. "It's Jake."

"Your brother's ringtone is a mariachi band?"

She slid up in bed, dragging the sheet with her. "He likes to dance." She clicked her phone and said, "Hey, Jake."

Her brother's voice came through the speaker. "Where are you?"

"I'm in Dublin… Actually, outside Dublin."

"Dublin! What are you doing in Ireland?

Mom's worried sick about you and it's no wonder. You're *not* home."

Sabrina laughed. "I'll be home tomorrow. I had something to do."

"What?"

She took a breath, glancing at Trent. He shrugged. Now that Pierre had been told there was no reason for secrecy anymore. He used that shrug to tell her he didn't see why she couldn't tell Jake about her baby.

"I had to tell Pierre that we were pregnant."

"What?" Jake's voice exploded from the phone.

Trent's eyebrows rose. Maybe he shouldn't have been so hasty in encouraging her to tell Jake.

"Look. It's all okay. I didn't want to tell anyone until I'd told Pierre and I told him two nights ago."

"That weasel is the father of your child?"

"He's the only guy I've been dating for the past four years. So, yes. He's the baby's father."

"Oh, hell."

"Don't worry. We're not going to do something foolish like get married. I told him that he could have as much or as little involvement with the baby as he wanted. But I also warned him that if he chooses to stay out of our child's life I'm giving our son or daughter his name when he or she reaches eighteen. What happens after that will be up to him or her."

Jake's voice softened. "You're really okay?"

She smiled at Trent. "I'm kind of excited. I've always wanted to be a mom. I know I'll get lots of support from you and Seth and Super Grandma." She gasped. "Hey, I haven't told Mom yet so just keep this between us."

"You know Avery will sense something and badger it out of me."

She laughed. "You can tell Avery. I'll tell Mom and Seth tomorrow."

"I'm glad you told me."

"I am, too." She glanced over at Trent again and she smiled. But he saw more than just her happiness. He'd experienced the closeness of the McCallan kids before, but hearing it first-hand tightened his chest. He couldn't imagine being this close to his half brother or sister, but he heard the sweetness of it in Sabrina's voice. He could tell she loved her brothers.

"So you're all by yourself in Dublin?"

"No." She looked at Trent again and he had the sense that this was something like a moment of truth. Would she tell her brother? And if she did, how would Jake react?

"Trent's with me."

His heart stuttered with relief.

"Trent?"

"I found out I was pregnant a few hours before Seth's wedding. Trent and I spent so much time together that day that I ended up telling him and he agreed to fly me to Paris, but Pierre wasn't there. So we went to Spain. Did you know Pierre has a huge working ranch?"

"The bastard."

"I know! He let us think he was a starving artist and all along he was... Well, maybe not rich, but at least solvent."

"He's a piece of work."

"Anyway, we found him in Dublin. I told him, and Trent and I headed for the airstrip, but we got caught in a rainstorm."

Jake's voice changed. "Rainstorm?"

"More like the end of a hurricane."

"Let me talk to Trent."

Sabrina handed her phone to Trent. "Jake wants to talk to you."

He fought an odd emotion that was sort of fear, but not normal fear, more like sheer panic that he'd have to explain his intentions to Sabrina's brother before he was even sure what Sabrina wanted.

As casual as possible, he took the phone and said, "Hey, Jake."

"If I'm on speaker, take me off."

"Okay." He clicked the button.

Jake said, "What's going on?"

"Exactly what Sabrina said. She needed help getting to Paris. I helped her. We'd be home right now except my assistant got the arrangements for a rental car wrong, then we drove right into this hurricane."

"Where are you?"

"We found an old castle. It looks like it was remodeled to be somebody's country house. I turned on the breaker, so we have electricity. But it almost doesn't matter now because I think we can leave for the airstrip this morning."

"Did you hear any of what happened with Pierre?"

Trent looked over at Sabrina and winked.

"You should have heard her. She laid down the law."

Jake laughed. "That's my sister."

"Yep. You can be proud of her."

"And you're okay with all this?"

Okay with all this? He might have found the love of his life…

But now was neither the time nor the place to tell Jake that, especially since he didn't really know if Sabrina agreed with him.

She'd wanted one night. He'd given it to her. Now he greedily wanted more. He wanted everything.

"It was my pleasure to help her. You know I owe you and Seth more favors than I can repay."

"You don't owe us any favors—"

"Of course I do. But I would have helped Sabrina anyway."

"Okay."

"Want to talk to Sabrina again?"

"No. You two just be safe."

"We will."

Trent hung up the phone, a strange feeling tapping on his brain. Jake never questioned that he and Sabrina had been alone in a house overnight. He never warned Trent away from her. He'd bet his last dollar that Sabrina's brother hadn't pictured them naked in bed as they spoke with him.

"Your brother really trusts you."

Apparently following Trent's line of thinking, Sabrina said, "Or he trusts you."

He caught her gaze, weird feeling after weird feeling rippling through him. He couldn't forget what it felt like to hold her, to kiss her, to be kissed by her. Everything with her was different, more intense, more meaningful. He'd already decided he'd give his entire fortune for a chance to explore it.

And he had no idea what Sabrina was thinking.

There was only one way to find out.

Staring into her pretty blue eyes, he said, "Or he thinks we'd make a good match."

He waited. Their gazes locked. The longing he'd erased from her eyes had been replaced by caution.

Still, her voice was soft and breathy when she said, "Maybe."

His heart slammed into his ribs. If they pursued this, they'd be taking a hell of a chance.

She was the baby sister of his friend. He had no idea how to be a good father…and she was pregnant.

Yet, it felt right.

Sabrina's phone burst out with a song Trent didn't recognize. His face must have registered his confusion because she said, "'Sunshine on My Shoulders.' My mom's a big John Denver fan."

He didn't know who John Denver was, so he only smiled, his thoughts going in and out and back and forth, his heart filled with something that felt a lot like hope…hope that wanted to spill over into joy.

"Hey, Mom."

As she listened to her mom talking, he almost stretched across the bed to nibble her shoulder, but he suddenly realized that she'd only been gone a few days, yet her mom had called twice. Her older brother had called once. If Seth hadn't been on his honeymoon, Trent was sure he would have called, too.

She took a deep breath, made the *shhh* sound with a finger to her lips, then hit the speaker button on her phone, giving him the chance to hear her mom's call the way he had Jake's.

His hope rose again. Was her including him in the calls a sign that she saw this relationship as more than one night?

"Then Jake calls me and says you're fine but you're in Dublin. Dublin! What are you doing in Dublin?"

"I went to see Pierre."

Trent's gaze leaped to Sabrina's.

She closed her eyes, took a deep breath and said, "I'm going to have a baby, Mom."

"What!"

"It's okay. I told Pierre that he could have as much or as little contact with our child as he wants but we both were very clear about the fact that we don't want to get married."

Her mom said nothing.

"I've always planned to be a mom."

"Yes, you have."

Though Sabrina's mom answered, her tone was stiff, formal.

"Don't be upset because my baby isn't coming after a big church wedding. We know Avery's having another girl. Maybe I'll have a boy."

Silence.

"Remember how you fawned over Seth and Jake? Imagine another little boy to spoil."

A laugh drifted from the phone. "Little boys can be such fun."

"And I'll need help. Maybe you should come over when I'm home and we can look at my spare room and see what we'd have to do to turn it into a nursery."

"We should hire a decorator."

Sabrina gave Trent a "watch this" expression. "I think you have good enough taste that you can do it without help."

Her mom laughed. "Are you buttering me up?"

"Maybe a little."

Maureen laughed again. "A baby."

"*Another* baby. You have Abby and Crystal, Avery's new little girl and now potentially a boy."

Maureen sighed. "We're blessed."

"Yes, we are."

Sabrina said, "Okay. I've got to go. You mull all that over and we'll talk when I get home. That should be tomorrow."

"How about if we have brunch together the day after?"

"That'd be great."

They said their goodbyes as Trent leaned against the headboard again. When she clicked off the call, he said, "Wow."

She laughed. "I wanted you to hear her panic because sometimes it's funny."

His heart warmed looking at her, seeing how much she loved her mother, remembering her affectionate conversation with Jake. Things he'd never had with his family. "You like to tease her."

"She's a hoot when she gets on a roll."

"I notice you didn't tell her about the hurricane."

"And have her hire mercenaries to try to rescue us?"

He chuckled. But he also realized she hadn't told her mom they were together. She'd told Jake, but not her mom.

"You really don't want her to worry."

"No. Not ever. We've had enough worry and pain in our lives."

That was when the closeness of the McCallan family came into sharp focus for Trent. Their father had been a tyrant. When he died, Jake found Avery and his life shifted enough that

Sabrina, Seth and their mom began to relax. Abby was born. Then Seth found Harper, who brought Crystal into their lives. Seth took the shaky steps to becoming a father and for the first time, the clan McCallan became a normal family.

Now Sabrina was bringing another child into their happiness. And the family would grow even tighter.

Unless *he* somehow botched everything.

He knew nothing about being a dad. And if he hurt Sabrina, he would hurt Jake and Seth and Maureen. He'd ruin the peace they'd finally found.

Thinking back to the terrified boy he'd met when Clark brought Seth to live in their apartment all those years ago, Trent stiffened. Living with their dad had been awful. Seth had confided many times. Though the McCallan patriarch had been gone for years, this was the first Trent had realized how much the family had changed. How happy they were...

And he could ruin their peace.

If he knew he could fit, if he knew what he felt for Sabrina would be strong enough to endure his mistakes, he wouldn't hesitate.

But he was a misfit. He couldn't guarantee anything. Except maybe failure. For as much as he'd always said that his stepfather had never warmed up to him, there were two people in that equation. What if it hadn't been his stepfather's fault? What if it had been his fault? What if he didn't know how to connect, how to love?

After all, he'd never had a girlfriend that he'd stayed with longer than a few months.

And the price for failure here was Sabrina's happiness. The contentment she'd found in becoming a mom. The peace of her close family.

Sabrina slid down in the bed and half turned to nestle against him. He shifted away, rolling to get out of bed.

"Do you hear that?"

She lifted her head, paid attention. "I don't hear anything."

"That's just it. There's no drumming rain, no whipping wind. The rain stopped last night but now the wind is gone, too. I'm going to get dressed, maybe take the SUV up the road a few miles to check out the damage."

She shook her head. "We have all day."

"Not really."

Her face scrunched with confusion. "Trent?"

"Look, maybe we made a mistake last night."

"Two seconds before my brother called, you were on the verge of suggesting a relationship."

"Yeah. I was." Her boldness shamed him, but it was also her happiness—the hard-won happiness of her entire family—that made his decision. He stepped into the black pants from the tux he'd had on the night before, then faced her. "You and I have always been honest."

She held his gaze.

"So I'm going to continue that."

She nodded again, but her eyes clouded with confusion that almost did him in. His choice was to hurt her now or devastate her later.

"In the past forty years, your family hasn't had a lot of happiness."

Her face shifted. Her lips lifted into a warm smile and her eyes lit with joy. "We do now."

He sat on the edge of the bed. "Do you understand why?"

"I think my brothers finding love changed things."

"What if they'd picked the wrong mates?"

"If they hadn't married Avery and Harper?"

"If they'd married women who didn't fit into your family."

"They didn't."

"Pretend they did. Pretend they married someone your mom didn't like…" He stopped, slowly met her gaze. "Someone who wasn't a good mom to your mother's precious grand-children."

"They're both great moms."

"But what if they weren't? What if they hurt your family dynamics?"

She searched his gaze before she said, "Like your stepdad."

"Yeah."

"What are you saying?"

"Your family is finally happy. Finally solid. It never dawned on me until I heard Jake's voice and your mom's voice just how fragile all this is for you."

"It's not fragile—"

"It is. You just don't see it."

She stiffened. "Because I'm not a romantic the way most women are?"

"No. Because you were right all along. A relationship between us is a bad idea. Not because one of us is bad or good…but because your whole life is going to change and so is your family's and I'm not the guy to take a chance with at this point."

She reached for him. "Trent—"

He caught her hand, kissed the palm. "This is about securing your family's happiness but it's also about me. If we fail, and there's a good chance we will, your family isn't the only ones who will get hurt. I will, too."

Her eyes softened. "And you've already been hurt enough."

"Exactly." He said it softly, quietly, so angry with fate and himself and his upbringing and his shortcomings that he could have punched a wall, but he stayed calm, logical, because reason was the language she understood.

"And we've been together four days." He squeezed the hand he held. "A relationship is a fun thought. A wonderful possibility. But we haven't gotten in so deep that we know it will work, or that we can't back out before we make a mistake."

Sabrina stared at him. He was the most intuitive person she'd ever met yet he hadn't seen that it was already too late. Making love the night before had gotten her in too deep. She wouldn't have melted under his touch, given herself to him the way she had, as she never had with any other man, if she hadn't already fallen in love. She simply hadn't known it until they'd gone the whole way and her heart had lifted, and her soul had sighed with the relief of finally finding real love.

She slid away and took the sheet with her as she rose. "I get it."

"Do you?"

She nodded, pasted a smile on her face. "Sure. What we had was a one-night stand and all that. Besides—" she pointed at her belly "—I'm kind of going to be busy for the next nine months and eighteen years."

"Yeah." He returned her smile. "And you're going to make a great mom."

But she wouldn't make a great wife. She was so damaged that a man with his own problems couldn't take a chance on her. She wanted to kick herself for being foolish enough to romanticize what was happening between them when really it was nothing.

Her heart shattered into a million pieces. She knew better.

She'd always known the idea of real love was untrustworthy.

But she'd been so sure. Not of herself…of him.

And he didn't want her.

Pain flooded her. Her chest ached. Her limbs felt like they wouldn't support her. "You know, I think I'll shower and dress while you check out the roads."

He rose from the bed. "Okay. I'll be back in twenty minutes."

She had to work to keep her voice from shivering when she said, "I'll be ready."

In the shower she tried to tell herself that it was better to be dumped after a one-night stand than to be married to someone for years before their true colors emerged. But it didn't stop the tears.

She'd trusted him. She'd fallen in love with him.

And he didn't want her.

When she was done dressing, she remembered the mess they'd made in the great room and cleared the table, tossed the burned-down candles, put the empty bottles in the trash.

She'd tried to do it clinically, tried to do it

without remembering what dancing with him felt like, without remembering the slow, delectable kisses that she'd thought were filled with emotion. But everything came back to her…the emotion. The longing. The need. The fulfillment.

She forced herself to stop seeing herself and Trent and began imagining the Irish couple. She disappeared. Trent disappeared. And the happy Irish man and woman with the kids filling the upstairs beds and the servants tucked away in the quarters were the man and woman who danced.

By the time Trent returned to tell her the roads were clear, she could pretend she was fine. But on the drive to the airstrip she texted her assistant to arrange to have a car pick her up at the airport in New York. She didn't talk to Trent on the flight and when the plane landed she walked directly to the McCallan limo that awaited her.

She didn't say goodbye.

She left him with his phone to his ear, back to doing the job that he loved.

CHAPTER THIRTEEN

MONDAY MORNING TRENT awoke in his Upper East Side condo. Two stories, it boasted a commercial-grade kitchen, a wine room, a master suite fit for royalty and exclusive access to the roof. He filled a mug with coffee, threw a robe over his sweatpants and baggy T-shirt and climbed the two flights of stairs that took him to his haven.

Three conversation areas with outdoor sofas and chairs and glass stone fire pits sat on bright aqua area rugs. He walked to the edge, where a five-foot Plexiglas wall served as a barrier, leaned over to watch the sun rise…

And felt nothing.

Except anger with himself.

How could he have been so stupid as to seduce a woman who was off-limits? He had legendary self-control. He could analyze any situation and know—with absolute certainty—

if it was good or bad, right or wrong, yet he'd forgotten important parts of the equation when adding his life to Sabrina's. She had a family, a real family who loved her. Family who would help her with her baby. Family who would give her baby the peace of belonging.

And he came with nothing. Except money. A little power. A lot of emptiness.

With a huff of anger, he turned from the spectacle in the sky and went back inside. There was no way he could take all this emotion to one of his lake houses. Being alone with this anger? With his self-recrimination? That wouldn't work.

What he needed to do was go into the office.

Talk to his staff.

Get back his sense of self.

And forget about soft blue eyes filled with longing...that he'd satisfied. Almost as if they were supposed to be together.

Calling himself an idiot, he gulped the coffee in his mug, jogged down the stairs to the master suite, showered, dressed and was in the back of his town car in under an hour. After a brief "Good morning" and an exchange about the beautiful end-of-August day, silence descended in the plush vehicle. He pulled his phone from his breast pocket and started reading newspapers.

Twenty minutes later he entered the building housing his offices, leaving the noise of Manhattan traffic behind. The ping of his private elevator announced his arrival at his office, so he wasn't surprised to see Ashley, a pretty twenty-seven-year-old in the process of getting her MBA, and Makenzie standing at attention, ready to work.

"Ladies," he greeted as he strode to his desk.

They scurried to follow him. "Good morning, Trent."

"I've texted a list of articles I want you to print out for me."

Makenzie looked confused. "Print out?"

He wasn't about to tell his staff that he was experimenting with different work habits to use his brain in a different way, so it wouldn't have time to slide over to Sabrina, to wonder where she was, what she was doing, if she was hurt or angry or both.

"Yes. Print out."

Makenzie looked about to argue, but Ashley gave her head a quick shake, a warning to the newbie she was training not to question the boss.

He rattled off a litany of instructions, watching Makenzie furiously taking notes as Ashley nodded.

But when Makenzie left the room, Ashley didn't follow her out. She closed the door behind her and turned to Trent.

"Are you okay?"

He didn't look up from his desk. "Why wouldn't I be?"

"Being stranded in a tropical storm and having to stay in someone else's house, waiting for roads to reopen, with a woman who is something of a stranger can't be fun."

But it had been fun. Some of the most fun of his life. He'd never felt more connected to another person. Never felt that complete.

"We considered ourselves lucky to find shelter and even luckier that it had canned food in a pantry."

"Canned food?"

"Peas, corn…" He shrugged. "Spam."

She laughed. "Spam?"

"I'll have you know I made a fantastic goulash."

Which Sabrina had loved. She hadn't laughed at his knowledge of the easy, low-cost meal. She never put on airs. She'd had the same empty ache in her soul that he had. Almost as if they'd been searching for each other.

Damn it! He had to stop thinking like that.

"Anyway, I have a lot of things to do today."

"I thought you were taking a week at the lake to unwind."

"My time in Ireland was my downtime. Now I need to work."

Ashley nodded and left, closing the door behind her. He tossed his pen to his desk. If he let himself, he would remember every second of his time with Sabrina, every word she'd said, how different it had been to make love with her.

So he couldn't let himself.

But the second he forced away thoughts of Sabrina, emptiness filled him, along with the sense that the life he was so sure gave him purpose and meaning was actually a sham.

Sabrina pressed a button on her security pad and opened her condo door for her mother. Maureen walked in, her face glowing, her eyes shining. She caught Sabrina in a huge hug and squeezed so hard, Sabrina thought she'd break a rib.

"I'm so happy that you're going to be a mom."

"Me, too." She said the words brightly, but inside her heart was broken. Her soul shivered as if it had taken a beating and lost part of itself. "Would you like some coffee?"

Maureen held up a bag. "Yes. That would go very nicely with one of these cinnamon bagels. I know we'd talked about going to brunch but I'm too eager to get a crack at turning your guest room into a nursery."

When Sabrina had a bottle of water and her mom had a cup of coffee with refills in a silver service complete with cream and sugar, they walked to the sofa and chair.

Setting the silver tray on the coffee table, Maureen said, "So how are you feeling?"

"Good. Great, actually." She winced. "No morning sickness like Avery seems to get."

Her mother beamed. "Oh, lucky you!" She bit into her bagel and groaned with delight. "So good."

Sabrina swallowed the bite of bagel she'd taken. "The best in the city."

"So you're feeling okay..."

"Yes, but I need to be at the top of my game. An easy pregnancy will make it possible for me to get done all the things I have to do to be able to take time off work when the baby is born, as I create a nursery and playroom."

Finished with her bagel, Maureen rubbed her hands together. "No time like the present. Do you have a tape measure?"

"Yes." Sabrina walked to the kitchen island to get it. "Thanks, Mom. I really appreciate your help."

Especially when she was drowning in a loss so deep and so profound she wasn't sure she could decorate a box, let alone a nursery and playroom. But even as she had that thought, she realized Trent couldn't call his mom and ask for help. He couldn't call her to share his pride over his successes or even to wish her merry Christmas.

It hurt her heart to think about it, but she reminded herself that his awful past had limited his ability to have a real relationship as much as hers had. If anything, the terrible way they'd ended things had proven she'd been right all along. There was no such thing as real love.

She fought to keep her eyes from filling with tears. There might not be any such thing as real love but oh, how she'd wanted it to be real. Trent hadn't shown her a fairy tale. He'd shown her how two people who genuinely cared for each other could be good to each other. But that didn't mean it was without passion and romance. No man had ever made her feel giddy with delight or weak with longing. If she had one wish for the world it would be that those feelings could be sustained—

That people really could be connected.

That people really could care for each other forever.

That making love could be as warm and wonderful as what she'd felt with him.

That mornings after could be filled with love and laughter and a closeness that brought contentment and peace.

Until her family had called.

Though Trent had proven that those things exist, he'd also shown her that they couldn't be sustained and now she had to reenter the real world.

A little smarter.

A little stronger.

But a hell of a lot sadder.

She led her mom back to the second bedroom, her heart heavy. She might be pragmatic about what had happened, but it still hurt. If she hadn't arranged for her mom to help redecorate, she might not have gotten out of bed that morning. She might not have ever gotten out of bed at all.

She took the rest of the week off to scout wallpaper and flooring with her mom. After a long, lonely weekend, she arrived at her office on Monday morning to find the invitation to the annual fall charity ball had arrived while she was in Europe. She marked the RSVP as attending, told her assistant, Maria, to send it back and settled in her desk to work.

But thoughts of dancing in Barcelona came back to her like a punch in the stomach, followed by memories of dancing in the Irish castle's great room. If she closed her eyes she could feel Trent's arms around her.

Combing her fingers through her hair, she rose from her desk chair and turned to the view of Manhattan visible through the enormous window behind her work area.

She'd gotten herself to the point where she

could keep her brain from thinking about Trent, or wishing things were different, but memories of little things invaded her thoughts all the time.

It might be because she'd found the blue sparkly dress in her luggage and couldn't quite get herself to donate it to charity. It might be because she'd begun leaving her hair natural because she really did like it that way.

No matter that Trent had hurt her, she'd found a piece of herself when she was with him. So when she returned to her desk to finish the mail and found the bill for the blue gown she'd bought in Dublin, she picked up her cell phone and dialed the number for the shop.

"I'm Sabrina McCallan. You probably don't remember me, but I bought a blue gown from you a little over a week ago. While I was there I tried on a red gown, too. I don't recall the designer, but it was a long-sleeved, form-fitting dress with no back."

The clerk said, "Ah. I know the dress you're talking about."

"I have a ball in two weeks. I'd like to wear

that dress. Can I order it from you and have it shipped to New York?"

"Absolutely."

She gave the clerk her size and then full name and address for delivery. As sad and empty as she sometimes felt, she *had* found herself on that trip. That was the part of the experience she had to remember. She'd get the dress that made her feel like her real self to push forward another step.

She might forever mourn the loss of what she'd had with Trent, but she needed to move on, and what better way to help herself move on than by letting herself be the person she'd found that week.

Trent entered the Annual Fall Ball two weeks later, two steps behind Seth and Harper. He'd spoken with Seth a few times since returning from Ireland and Seth hadn't mentioned Sabrina. Apparently, she'd kept what had happened between them to herself.

He tapped Seth's shoulder and when Seth turned around to see him, he grinned. "Hey!" He clasped Trent's hand before bringing him in for the quick shoulder bump.

"Good to see you guys," he said to both Harper and Seth. "How's married life?"

Seth said, "Couldn't be better," and Harper laughed. "He's discovering that he likes cooking."

"Just stupid things like macaroni and cheese that Crystal likes."

"He's actually started texting helpful hints to Sabrina, though her baby won't be able to eat food like this for a good two years."

Seth laughed, and Trent's heart tumbled. He yearned to ask Seth how Sabrina was, if she'd been sick, if she was back to work…if she missed him, but he knew Seth would read into his eagerness and start making guesses. If Sabrina hadn't wanted her family to know something had happened while they were traveling, he didn't want to say the thing that tipped them off.

He also didn't want to seem like a lovestruck puppy. He was getting beyond what had happened between them. He really was. He'd actually hoped they'd see each other tonight, hold a decent conversation and maybe put a period at the end of the sentence of the story of them.

He drifted away from Seth and Harper and was drawn into a conversation with two bankers. He managed to get away from them to chat with a few real estate guys before he finally found his table. His seatmates were from two families with old money. He took the opportunity to pick the brain of the patriarchs—a person could never have too much knowledge about markets and industry—but a flash of red caught his eye.

He stopped talking and glanced over to see Sabrina, wearing a red gown, her hair down and a little wild.

She turned to take her seat at the McCallan table and he gasped. There was no back on the dress. It dropped to a spot just above her perfectly shaped bottom.

Memories of touching her, tasting her, assaulted him. If he'd been holding a fork, he would have dropped it. In the thirty seconds he stared at her, he knew why he was having so much trouble forgetting her... He didn't want to.

But looking at that dress, he realized it was *the* dress. Her declaration of independence dress. She was done following rules—

No. She was making her own rules.

The way he used to…

His gaze moved from her to her brother Seth and lovely Harper, to Jake and savvy Avery, to their mom… Maureen, a tower of strength.

Something shuffled through his mind so quickly he couldn't process it. He gave the entire family another once-over and realized what he'd seen…

They were fine. They were strong. Beside Avery, Jake looked invincible. Sitting next to Harper, Seth grinned in a way Trent had never seen before. Her red dress a symbol of her new sense of self, Sabrina glowed.

So did Maureen. She'd spent forty years in a bad marriage, protecting her children, but that was over.

No one would ever hurt this family again.

Not even him.

They'd fought for this life and they wouldn't let anyone or anything snatch it away from them again.

Realization brought him to his feet. *They* were fine. Strong. Happy. *He* wasn't. The only thing keeping him from Sabrina was his fear that he would ruin the McCallans. Now that he knew he wouldn't, he saw the other side of his dread. The *reason* he'd drawn the conclusions he had.

Sabrina had faced down her demons on her trip to tell Pierre— No. Trent had forced her to face her demons when he hadn't faced his.

He didn't fully understand what had happened between him and his stepdad but he did know he couldn't have an honest relationship with anyone until he did.

He took a breath. He belonged with Sabrina. But not with the questions hanging over his head.

It was time to figure this out.

He rose, said his goodbyes and walked into the lobby of the grand hotel. He pulled out his phone to call his driver and in five minutes his car was at the entrance. The driver opened his door and once he was settled he gave him the address of his parents' home.

CHAPTER FOURTEEN

TRENT ARRIVED AT the two-story frame house. Trimmed hedges, a neat walkway to the front door and newly painted black trim against white siding said this was the home of a proud working-class family.

He headed up the walk to the black front door with the etched glass center panel. Though it was after ten o'clock at night, he rang the bell.

The door opened. His mother's jaw fell when she saw him, but he also noticed that her dark eyes lit with unguarded happiness.

She reached out to hug him. "Trent."

"Mom." He returned her hug, closing his eyes when emotion threatened to overwhelm him. They'd been a team for years after his father's death. He'd never been closer to another person. To have been away from her for three long years, suddenly seemed absurd.

He pulled back, opening his eyes, and saw his tall, slim stepfather. "Jim."

"Humph. Not Dad anymore?"

He wanted to remind Jim that he was the one who had run him off, refused a gift, made Trent feel he'd somehow wronged him, insulted him… That was after decades of being made to feel he didn't belong, didn't fit.

His mother wrung her hands and nervously said, "How about some cake and coffee?"

His stepfather scowled. "Don't be going to any trouble for him."

That was the attitude that had always made him feel less than, unwelcome. But today he saw it for what it was. Just as Sabrina had known Pierre was a narcissist, Trent finally saw his stepfather was a grouch. He might not have reached the heights of Jake, Seth and Sabrina's dad, but they were cut from the same cloth.

Today Trent simply wasn't going to be moved by him.

"Actually, Mom, I'd like a piece of cake." He smiled at her. "And some coffee."

"Coming right up!"

She scurried off and Trent didn't wait for his

stepfather to invite him into the living room that had been part of the home his mom had owned when she married Jim. He slid by him, saying, "Why don't you and I have a bit of a talk while the coffee brews."

"What? You think you're going to put me down or make fun of me while your mom's out of the room?"

Seriously? For the first time in his life, Trent saw that his stepfather had some real issues. He slipped off his tux jacket and sat on the worn, but comfortable sofa.

"You know what, Jim? For decades you made me feel unwanted and tonight I finally see that maybe I shouldn't have accepted that."

His stepfather's mouth tightened.

"I was a kid. A little boy who needed a dad and you were…" He hesitated to say it, but if they were going to get this out in the open and deal with it, he had to say it. "You were jealous of me."

"I wasn't jealous of you. You were bad."

He shook his head. "No. I wasn't. I remember being so excited to get a dad. I would have been anything, *done* anything you wanted. But you shut me down." He drew in a breath. "But none of that matters. I'm here to say the past is the past. You may not want to, but I think we should start over. I love my mother. I miss her and I miss Jamie and Pete, too. They're my family."

Jim squirmed a bit on his seat.

"And I want them back. You can join us when we have dinner or go to a show or even vacation together. Actually, I think it would be fun for all of us to rent a big house in Key West. We could hire someone to take us fishing. But if you want to stay home I've decided that's *your choice*."

Sounding old and tired, Jim said, "Your mother's not going to want to go on fancy vacations or to shows—"

"Of course I am." His mother strode into the living room, carrying a tray with three plates holding huge slices of chocolate cake, the coffeepot and three mugs. "I never did understand what happened when Trent bought us that house. Except that you said you didn't want it and Trent left without another word. I'd hoped it would iron itself out. Since it didn't I'm glad Trent's here, so we can fix it."

Jim rolled his eyes. "This is stupid." He strode to the stairway. "I'm going to bed."

Continuing with his decision to let Jim either join them or not, his choice, Trent said, "Good night, Jim."

He stopped, turned and shook his head as if realizing he might as well not fight this. "Good night."

It wasn't much, but it was a start. His mom handed Trent a piece of cake as Jim disappeared up the stairway.

"I think he's afraid of you."

Trent shook his head. "No. I think he's afraid of change."

"He's old-fashioned and he's proud."

Trent glanced around the tidy home. "He has a lot to be proud of. I respect him and what you guys have. But he has nothing to fear from me." He took his mother's hand and squeezed it. "I just missed you."

"I missed you, too." She smiled at Trent. "And I'm so sorry. I always noticed things were different with you and Jim. I just didn't know how to handle it."

"We're fine, Mom. I think all of us hoped

it would smooth out on its own. Because it didn't, we're fixing it now."

His new rules began to form in his head. "One night a month I can either visit here or take you to dinner and a show."

"That would be nice."

"Holidays I can come here until Sabrina and I get established."

"Who is Sabrina?"

He laughed. "Someone who might throw a ring back in my face if I get the proposal wrong."

His mother gasped. "You're getting married?"

"Not right away." He winced. "Technically, we haven't even dated but watching her handle a big problem that had come up in her life I suddenly realized I'd been running from mine." He shrugged. "And that's not who I am."

"No. You were never a runner. You always jumped right in and faced things."

"But I didn't know how to handle Jim."

"I think you do now."

"I think I do, too."

They ate cake and drank coffee and talked

about anything and everything. He didn't say much more about Sabrina. He'd taken a huge leap involving her in his future when she might not want a damned thing to do with him and he didn't blame her.

But the woman with the problem had taught the man who thought he didn't have any problems how to take a closer look and be a little more honest with himself.

She wasn't just a beautiful face with the great figure and a mind like a steel trap. She made him a better person and he wanted her in his life.

He just had to figure out the proposal she wouldn't be able to resist.

Sabrina McCallan stood by the huge double doors, looking at the castle outside Dublin, formal invitation in hand. The invite said the charity was having a showing of *her* paintings, but she hadn't realized it would be held at *the* castle where she and Trent had taken shelter from the rain—

And there were no cars for other guests. There was no line of limos dropping off dignitaries and society matrons. There was just her and the moonlight.

She'd checked into the charity and it was legitimate. They'd been thrilled she was planning to attend and were eager for the money from the showing—

Still, being here right now, it all seemed a bit odd.

As her driver maneuvered the big limo down the circular driveway to the road at the bottom of the hill, a case of nerves assaulted her. She opened her shiny black purse to get out her phone and call her car back, because the whole thing was beginning to feel like the first scene of a horror movie, but the double doors of the entry opened.

A man in tails greeted her. "Good evening, Ms. McCallan."

She took a breath. Would a serial killer go to this much trouble to get her alone?

Yes. Damn it.

"I'm sorry but I think there was some sort of mix-up here." Her phone in her hand, she stretched her thumb to call her driver.

The butler said, "Mr. Sigmund has been awaiting you."

She froze. Trent? She missed him in a way she'd never missed anyone because she'd let herself fall in love with him, and he'd rejected her. Now he'd lured her back to the castle where he'd hurt her?

The butler bowed at the waist, motioning for her to come inside. Though her first instinct was to reject Trent the way he'd rejected her, curiosity got the better of her.

She shouldn't be giving him the time of day. He'd hurt her more than anyone ever had. Not because leaving her had been so devastating but because until she'd met him she hadn't believed love existed. He'd shown her it did then took it all back. Leaving her alone, disillusioned and in the kind of emotional pain she'd managed to avoid for twenty-eight years.

As the butler led her through the first sitting room and into the more formal living room, she realized the place was clean.

Sparkling clean.

She glanced around, breathless with awe. Even in need of a good remodel the castle was amazing. A home. Not like the McCallan family's three-story condo where her mom hosted holidays or the mansion in Montauk, but a real home. With fires in the fireplaces and the scent of cinnamon as if someone had baked cookies.

A case of warm fuzzies overwhelmed her and she let them because they felt right. Something about this castle had always called to her.

"Sabrina…"

Trent walked over to her, his hands extended to take hers. His hair was short, the way he'd had it cut the last time they were in Dublin. He looked rich and powerful and sinfully sexy, but also warm and wonderful. Just the touch of his hands filled her heart with happiness.

But he'd also dumped her—

She pulled her hands from his and waved the engraved invitation. "I thought this was an exhibition. I called the charity, verified the facts."

"I gave them a ton of money to host this without hosting it. And it is an exhibition." He pointed to three of her paintings hanging on the wall to the right. "They just happen to be paintings that I own."

"You bought my paintings?"

"I would buy all of your paintings if it weren't

so impractical and selfish." He glanced lovingly at a huge picture of a little blonde girl in a meadow. "I think that one's a self-portrait."

It was. But not in the conventional sense. She'd painted herself in a beautiful meadow, but alone. She'd always been surrounded by beauty, but she'd also been very much alone.

She suddenly realized this castle was the first place she hadn't felt alone, the first place she'd let herself be herself.

And he knew that.

"This whole deal feels kind of sleazy and cheap."

He arched a brow. "Let me assure you. It was not cheap."

"You know what I mean."

"I do." He turned and led her through the sitting room to a corridor she didn't remember to the great room. "But I knew it was going to take a grand gesture not just for you to hear me out, but to understand."

The table was set with the good china. Candles burned between the two catty-corner places.

The need to cry shivered through her. In the weeks that had passed, she'd barely let herself think about the night they'd spent here. And now here it was, recreated for her.

He lifted the lid off a silver bowl and the scent of his goulash floated out.

Tears filled her eyes, but she laughed. "What are you doing?"

"Apologizing." He stuffed his hands in his trouser pockets. "Explaining."

After the first week had gone by without a word from him, she'd dashed any hope that he might have acted hastily or made a mistake. She'd spent every day since then working to get over him. But one bowl of goulash, one sweet gesture, and she was butter.

"I let you go because I was afraid I would hurt the fragile peace your family had just established."

"So you said."

"But I saw your family at the charity ball a few weeks ago. I saw that you're all strong. Even your mom. And I thought it was a little vain of me to think I could hurt you."

"It was." But she had understood it. Even two years after her dad's death, she was still cautious, still afraid. It had taken four days with Trent for her to see she'd been living in a prison.

"Don't forget, I'd carried the guilt of ruining one family." He took a breath. "So I paid a visit to my mom and stepdad and realized I hadn't really ruined anything. My stepdad's a piece of work, frequently grouchy, but I think he's hiding a low self-esteem."

"Oh, yeah?"

He motioned for her to come to her seat and she did—slowly—as hope built inside her. A man who'd bought her paintings and arranged to meet her in the house where they'd fallen in love had to have something important to say.

He pulled out her chair and helped seat her, then took the chair across from the candles.

"You look lovely. Even if you are playing it safe with blue."

She laughed. "You didn't think I'd wear the backless dress to an event where I knew no one."

"I thought you were bold."

Her gaze jumped to his. "I am bold. I came to this castle only out of curiosity—" She stopped, cleared her throat. "I didn't even realize this was the castle we were forced to stay in."

"I bought this place."

Shocked, she glanced around. "You did?"

"For us. It was a matter of looking at public records to find the owner, but he wasn't willing to sell until I told him our story." He laughed. "Then he welcomed my offer with open arms. A few decades ago, he'd bought this castle for his new wife. They'd summered here with their four kids. When I told him you were pregnant, he knew we'd keep this house a real home. That's what he wanted. That's what I want."

Her throat tightened with the longing to weep, and she swallowed. He'd barely explained himself, but he almost didn't have to. The story of the castle owner was the most romantic thing she'd ever heard. And what she needed from him was the romance she'd always believed didn't exist.

Still, she wanted that last little bit of confirmation. "For us?"

"We've known each other forever without really knowing each other, so though I brought a ring—"

She gaped at him.

"If you don't want to take it, I'll understand.

But no one has ever made me feel as wonderful as you do."

Emotion swelled in her chest, making it difficult to breathe, let alone think. She now knew romance was more than dancing and kissing. Honesty had brought them together. Only honesty would keep them together.

Her answer came straight from her heart. "No one's ever made me feel as wonderful as you make me feel, either."

"So we can take a few months or a few years." He shrugged. "Whatever we feel comfortable with before we get engaged."

Thoughts wound through her brain and eventually connected everything he was saying. "If that was a proposal you did a really poor job."

He laughed. "I chickened out."

"Why? You bought a castle! How can you chicken out at the best part? The part where you ask me to share it with you."

"Because the last time I saw you, you were still mad at me."

"The last time I saw you, you were naked. We were both naked. I could pick up right from that spot."

"You're not mad?"

"No. I understand. What happened between us happened fast. Now I see that you had some loose ends to tie."

He rose from his seat, sliding his hand into his jacket pocket and pulling out a black velvet ring box. Getting down on one knee, he opened the box and said, "Will you marry me?"

The tears she'd been fighting suddenly dried up. She pressed her lips together to stop a laugh before she said, "Yes."

Every crazy thing that had happened since the morning of Seth's wedding made sense.

After sliding the diamond on her finger, he took her hands and helped her to stand so he could kiss her.

"I feel like we're breaking about a thousand rules."

She laughed, lovingly looking at her diamond, then into his eyes. "Some people aren't made for rules. I spent my entire life trying to keep my dad's rules. Now I would just like to live my life." She smiled. "With you."

"Amen to that."

He kissed her again.

Then a maid arrived followed by the butler. When Trent and Sabrina were seated again, the butler poured sparkling apple juice. The maid brought warm rolls and soft butter. Their duties accomplished, they scurried away.

She gave him a confused look. "A butler and maid?"

He buttered a roll. "You said kids would be sleeping upstairs and servants would be in their first-floor quarters."

She laughed. "You really pay attention."

"It's one of my best traits."

She wanted to tell him about the Irish couple she'd seen in her fantasies about this house but suddenly realized they were the couple. They'd always been the couple because she'd always known she and Trent belonged together.

That was when she realized there really might be such a thing as women's intuition. She felt it right now. They might not live in this castle full-time. It might be their summer retreat, but no matter where they lived they'd be happy. Forever.

EPILOGUE

A LITTLE OVER eight months later, Sabrina lay in a hospital bed with Trent holding her hand and her doctor telling her to push.

She did.

When the push was over, her mother wiped sweat from her brow. "That's great, sweetie."

Trent kissed her forehead. "Really great."

The doctor peered at her above the sheet draped over her legs. "Okay. We're ready for another push. Make this one a good one."

She took a long breath, focused her gaze on Trent's encouraging face and pushed with all her might.

The doctor laughed and looked at her over the sheet again. "We have a girl."

Her mother gasped. "A girl? I thought you said you were having a boy?"

The doctor handed the baby to a nurse who scurried away. "We need some more pushes."

Trent squeezed her hand. "You're good. Just a few more pushes and we'll get that little boy."

Her mother gaped at Trent. "What boy? Another baby? Twins?" She looked down at Sabrina. "You knew you were having twins and you kept that from me?"

She glanced at her mom. "I wanted at least one surprise from this pregnancy."

"Push, Sabrina! Now!"

She pushed again, and again, and a third time, really hard.

"And here's our boy."

Maureen leaned down, peering over the sheet as if needing to confirm the second child. "How does a woman hide the fact that she's having twins…and from her mother!"

Sabrina sighed. "Are you or are you not surprised?"

"I'm shocked."

Trent laughed and peeked down at Sabrina. "From the look on her face I'd say that's true."

The nurse walked over with their baby girl. She handed her to Sabrina, who laughed through her tears. "Oh, my gosh!" She caught Trent's gaze. "We have two of these."

He kissed her forehead. "I know."

"Are you sure we can handle this?"

"I don't see why not. We do have two cribs in the castle and another one on order for the condo."

His condo. He had more space for a nursery, a playroom and nanny's quarters. All that remodeling had been done weeks ago. Now they'd start planning their wedding.

The nurse brought over their son. She would have handed him to Trent, but Sabrina insisted on switching. "Babies need to bond first with their mom." She handed Trent the little girl, then took the boy from the nurse.

"Hello, Sebastian."

Maureen raced to the other side of the bed and looked over Trent's shoulder. "Oh, she's beautiful. So tiny." She caught Sabrina's gaze. "And you knew she was coming?"

Sabrina laughed. "Yes, Mom. Her name is Selena." She paused a beat then said, "Want to go out to the waiting room and tell Seth and Jake it was twins?"

Maureen clapped. "Oh, this'll be fun!"

She raced to the door but stopped and faced Trent. "Your parents got here, didn't they?"

He'd flown them to Key West for a fishing

trip to celebrate his stepdad's retirement, not realizing Sabrina would go into labor early, and he'd had to send his jet back to retrieve them.

"They got here about two hours ago."

"Do they know about the twins?"

Trent stopped a laugh at her enthusiasm. Who would have ever thought the McCallan matriarch would love a good joke so much?

"Nope. Go have your fun."

She raced out of the room and Trent took his seat beside Sabrina's bed. "Are you okay?"

She cuddled Sebastian. "I'm so exhausted I could cry."

He laughed. "If what I'm told is true, we'd better get accustomed to that feeling."

Looking at her son, she smiled. "It'll be worth it."

He glanced at their little girl, already his in his eyes because he'd been with Sabrina since the day she'd discovered she was pregnant. "Yeah, it'll totally be worth it."

A round of laughter floated into the labor room from the hallway that led to the waiting room.

"I think your brothers like your joke."

"It wasn't a joke. It was a surprise. And every once in a while a family needs to be shaken up."

With a quick chuckle, he agreed. Once in a while, a family *did* need to be shaken up.

Since he'd met her, he'd reconciled with his family, bought a castle, remodeled his condo… become a dad and would soon be a husband.

Life didn't get any better than this.

* * * * *

LET'S TALK

Romance

For exclusive extracts, competitions
and special offers, find us online:

f facebook.com/millsandboon

⊙ @millsandboonuk

🐦 @millsandboon

Or get in touch on 0844 844 1351*

For all the latest titles coming soon,
visit millsandboon.co.uk/nextmonth

*Calls cost 7p per minute plus your phone company's price per
minute access charge

Want even more
ROMANCE?

Join our bookclub today!

'Mills & Boon books, the perfect way to escape for an hour or so.'

Miss W. Dyer

'Excellent service, promptly delivered and very good subscription choices.'

Miss A. Pearson

'You get fantastic special offers and the chance to get books before they hit the shops'

Mrs V. Hall

Visit millsandbook.co.uk/Bookclub and save on brand new books.

MILLS & BOON